Megan Parnell Mysteries

Mystery at Camp Galena

Mystery at Camp Galena

Joan Rawlins Biggar

CPH
SAINT LOUIS

Megan Parnell Mysteries

Missing on Castaway Island
Mystery at Camp Galena

Cover Illustration by Matthew Archambault.

Scripture quotations taken from the HOLY BIBLE, NEW INTERNATIONAL VERSION. NIV®. Copyright © 1973, 1978, 1984 by International Bible Society. Used by permission of Zondervan Publishing House. All rights reserved.

Copyright © 1997 Concordia Publishing House
3558 S. Jefferson Avenue, St. Louis, MO 63118-3968
Manufactured in the United States of America

Library of Congress Cataloging-in-Publication Data

1 2 3 4 5 6 7 8 9 10   06 05 04 03 02 01 00 99 98 97

Contents

Mystery at Camp Galena

s the school bus pulled to the curb in front of Madrona High, Megan Parnell grabbed her backpack and pressed after Peter into the bus aisle. "See you after school," she called to her stepbrother as they separated inside the school's front door.

Peter's blue eyes crinkled as he gave her a half-salute. His shining auburn head bobbed away through the crowd. Megan tossed her dark curls over her shoulder and maneuvered down a crowded side hall toward the locker she shared with Thuy Nguyen.

She found Thuy on tiptoe, reaching for a pen at the back of the locker's high shelf. "Hi, Megan!" Thuy bounced backward with the pen in hand. "Did you finish your essay last night?"

"Yes," Megan told her friend. "Why is it the first thing teachers want you to write about is what you did in the summer? Here we are, high school juniors, and we're still getting the same old assignment!"

Thuy laughed. "I didn't have a bit of trouble! I wrote about losing my brother on Whidbey Island and how you and Peter helped me find him."

"That's exactly what I wrote about," Megan exclaimed. "I called my story 'Castaway Island.'"

"I called mine 'Castaways'! Do you suppose Mrs. Jefferson will think we collaborated?"

"I hope not. If Peter were in honors English too, she'd really be suspicious, wouldn't she?"

They both laughed. Megan began to empty her backpack, piling her books into her locker. Someone banged the next locker's door into her back.

"Sorry!" It was Willow Elizabeth Hanes, the prettiest girl in honors English. Willow had a curvy figure, glossy brown hair swinging halfway down her back, and big green eyes. Last year she'd been one of the most popular girls in tenth grade.

Obviously she intended to carry on that tradition this year because instead of noticing that she'd knocked Megan and her armload of books off balance, she smiled at a passing boy.

Distracted by Willow's smile, the tall, blond boy paused in his stride. The people behind him dodged. One of them collided with Megan, who landed in a heap with her books on the floor.

"Are you all right?" A strong hand hauled her to her feet. Brilliant blue eyes smiled into hers. A broad white grin flipped her heart upside down as the blond boy scooped up her books and plopped them into her arms. "Okay?"

"Okay," Megan replied shakily. She watched his wide shoulders and the back of his golden head as he wove through the crowds of people heading for class. He was Sean Bertram, one of the student body leaders and a new member of her youth group at church. Every girl in school had a crush on him, and so did Megan, though she hadn't admitted it to anyone.

Her eyes came back to Willow Elizabeth, leaning against her locker and also watching the boy disappear.

Willow met her glance and shrugged. "Sorry," she said again.

"Here," Thuy said as the bell rang for class. "Your essay fell out of its folder."

"Thanks," Megan said, taking a quick look into the mirror inside their locker door. "If the rest of today goes like this," she muttered, "I'll never survive 'til school's out."

As she slipped into her seat, she tried to brush the print of someone's sneaker off the title page of her essay. In the next seat, Thuy saw what she was doing and handed her an eraser. Megan rubbed at the marks, then shook her head. She'd have to hand it in the way it was. At least it hadn't torn.

She placed her essay on the bottom of the stack as the papers came up the row, then settled back in her seat.

"I'll return these to you as soon as possible," Mrs. Jefferson told the class. She evened the papers and dropped them into a basket on her desk. "Before we begin this morning, I have an announcement. If you were in the Madrona Bay school system when you were a sixth-grader, you'll remember going to outdoor education camp.

"Because we're so close to the salt water, the outdoor school has been on Blue Island for some years. But the forests and mountains are also an important part of our environment here in the Pacific Northwest." Mrs. Jefferson pulled down a roller map of Washington state. "This fall all sixth-graders will be going to Camp Galena. It's a beautiful spot in the Cascades not far from here." She pointed.

Megan pricked up her ears. She, her mother, and their friends had often camped and hiked near Camp

11

Galena. Not this summer, which had been pretty much taken up with the wedding of her mom and Peter's dad. But other summers when they'd passed the camp, she'd wished they could stop and explore.

Mrs. Jefferson continued. "It's in the middle of old mining country, so campers will get to hike to old mines and learn more about pioneering days. Student counselors will be chosen from among qualified Madrona High students. If you think you'd like to counsel, there are meetings during both first and second lunches today." She handed out photocopied information sheets.

Megan scanned her sheet. She'd loved the three days she'd spent with her sixth-grade class on Blue Island. And she liked working with younger kids. Besides, as part of a newly blended family she felt as if she'd been walking on eggs for weeks, even though all of them—her mom, Peter, Peter's father, and she— were all trying valiantly to make the necessary adjustments. A few days away, where she didn't have to watch every word and action, would be wonderful. She leaned across the aisle to Thuy. "I'm going to that meeting," she whispered. "Are you interested?"

"Yes, but I can't be a counselor," Thuy whispered back. "The Youth Symphony is meeting almost every night. There's a concert coming up, you know."

"Oh, that's right." Thuy played the flute better than anybody Megan had ever heard.

At the front of the room, Mrs. Jefferson switched on the overhead projector. The buzz of conversation died as notebooks flipped open and their owners recorded the day's assignment.

At lunchtime Megan hurried to the multipurpose room, brown bag lunch in hand. As she entered the room, a familiar laugh stopped her in her tracks. "Peter?"

Peter's auburn head swiveled her way. "Hi, Megan. Are you here for the meeting?"

"Yes." So much for getting away from family. "I didn't expect to see you here."

Peter didn't seem to notice the coolness in her voice. "Jake had one of the information sheets. He invited me to tag along. Sounds like fun, doesn't it?"

Jake was in her honors class. She nodded to him. "Yeah. Well, talk to you guys after the meeting ..." She whirled around to look for a seat and banged into someone behind her. Her lunch bag flew through the air. That someone snagged it with a neat one-handed catch while with his other hand he caught her elbow and steadied her.

Bright blue eyes smiled down at her. Oh, no, Megan moaned to herself. Sean Bertram again!

"If we're going to keep running into each other like this, I'd better introduce myself," he said, returning her lunch bag.

"We've met," Megan said, blushing. "In youth group, remember? I'm Megan."

"Oh, sure ... I knew I knew you." Sean gave Peter the briefest of nods as his eyes flickered over the group gathering in the multipurpose room. "Looks like a nice crowd. Excuse me, I'm going to get a seat close to the front."

Megan couldn't look at Peter. Thank goodness he

had no idea she'd been dreaming about Sean for the past month or more. Obviously Sean hadn't been dreaming about *her*.

Willow arranged herself in a graceful pose as Sean walked by. Megan wrinkled her nose, then took an empty seat beside Peter and Jake and unwrapped her sandwich.

One of the school officials explained the outdoor education program and what was expected of the student counselors. There would be further meetings for those accepted into the program, he said. Most students stayed to fill out the forms and mark the sessions they'd like to attend.

Willow finished and got up to take her form to the official. She stopped by Megan's seat, eyeing Peter flirtatiously. "Is this your boyfriend, Megan?"

"Boyfriend?" Megan glanced at Peter with a little laugh. "No. This is my stepbrother, Peter Lewis. You know Willow, don't you, Peter?"

Peter nodded hello, looking dazzled as Willow aimed a smile his way and asked, "Which class are you in, Peter?"

"I'm a junior, same as Megan."

"No, I mean which honors class?"

Peter's ears reddened. "No honors class. I'm just your average, run-of-the-mill student."

"Oh," said Willow. "I was under the impression that only the best ... I mean, the top ..." She fumbled to a halt. "Well, anyway, which session did you sign up for?"

"The first one."

"Me too." Willow looked past Peter, surveying the

people moving about the room. Her eyes fastened on Sean in the center of a knot of students. "See you." Application in hand, she glided toward the counselor in a route that took her past Sean.

Megan watched Willow go, her mouth drawn into a straight line. Her dark eyes flashed. "Honestly! As if being in honors class is the only measure of a person's worth!" Forgetting her desire to get away from family, she erased the "third session" she'd penciled in on her application and wrote "first session" instead. If Peter wanted to be a counselor, she'd be there to support him, whether Willow thought him good enough or not.

~~~~~~~~~~~~~~~~~~~~

A few days later, both Megan and Peter found their names on the list of people chosen to be counselors. On Saturday morning, Megan's mom signed the permission slips for them to be part of the program and told Megan she could drive the van to the counselors' training meeting. When Megan and Peter walked into the high school's multipurpose room, they saw a few students chatting in small groups. One or two sat in the chairs in front of the stage. "Where is everybody?" Peter asked.

"We're early," Megan answered. "But that's okay. We can get a good seat."

"Save me one," he said. "I see someone I want to talk to."

A girl Megan didn't know sat alone in the front row. She seemed young for high school, and her freckled face, framed with short brown curls, looked scared. Megan felt sympathetic. "Hi," she said. "Okay if I sit beside you?"

A surprised smile lit the girl's eyes. "Sure. Sit down."

Megan put her notebook on the next chair to save it for Peter. "I'm Megan," she said. "Are you going to be a counselor?"

"Megan? I'm Jodi Marsh." Jodi smiled again and relaxed a little. "I'm only in the ninth grade, so I can't be a counselor yet. But they asked me to come tell you about part of this year's program for Camp Galena."

"Oh? What part?"

"There's an old miner's cabin and a mine in Morning Gulch. It's near Camp Galena ... close enough for the kids to hike to ..."

"Really? I've hiked quite a bit up in those mountains, but I've never been to Morning Gulch."

"The trail wasn't in very good shape until this last year, so not many people know about it. My brother and cousin and I found the old cabin when we got caught in a storm. It was just like the owners had left it."

"That must have been exciting!"

"It was. And I found a letter written by Lucy Steincroft, the little girl who had lived there. She'd hidden it in her treasure bag. Then her father died in a mine cave-in and she and her mother left in such a hurry she forgot to take it."

A treasure bag? A forgotten letter? Intriguing! Megan scarcely noticed the students filling up the seats around them. "What did the letter say?"

"Well, it said Lucy's father found gold ... some was in the bag with the letter. And it told about the accident that killed him. But the most interesting part came when we got back to Bayview, where we live. The boys and I found Lucy Steincroft. She was an old lady by then, of course. We got to be good friends ..."

A screech from the microphone interrupted them. As the program director called for attention, Peter slipped into the seat Megan had saved for him. They both took notes in their counselor's handbooks as the director spoke about the camp and the outdoor education program. A sixth-grade teacher went over the list of counselor's responsibilities in their handbooks. Megan tried to listen but her mind kept flying back to her interrupted conversation with Jodi. Was the gold mine still there? Did Lucy ever go back to Morning Gulch?

Then the program director took the microphone again. "Part of our curriculum at outdoor school includes learning about the early history of the surrounding area. Starting in the 1880s, prospectors combed the mountains around Camp Galena, searching for precious minerals. This morning, to tell you more about that, we have a guest from our neighboring town, Bayview."

Megan glanced at Jodi, who looked pale. Megan patted her hand and whispered, "You'll do a great job."

Jodi took a deep breath. "Thanks," she whispered back.

"Jodi Marsh and her brother and cousin discovered an old miner's cabin near Camp Galena," continued the director. "It was her idea to get the cabin and the nearby mine restored for the public to enjoy. Because of Jodi's hard work, we will be able to give our campers an experience to remember.

"Come on up, Jodi, and tell us about your adventure."

The students clapped politely as Jodi climbed to the

stage and the director handed her the microphone. Megan saw her gulp and duck her head for a moment, as if asking for courage. Then she shakily began her story.

Her voice grew stronger as she told of her cousin Billy's frightening tumble into a storm-swollen creek and of finding the abandoned cabin where they took shelter for the night. She talked about the clues that helped them find the elderly Lucy Steincroft and solve the mystery of her father's hidden gold.

Megan almost forgot to breathe as Jodi told about the old miner, Jack McCracken. In his attempt to frighten them away from the mine, he'd accidentally trapped the boys ... and Jodi had to go down a deep air shaft, in spite of her fear of closed-in places, to find them. "I prayed hard," Jodi said. "I was never so scared ... not even when they asked me to come talk to you today!"

The students laughed. They listened intently as she told of Lucy's wish that the old cabin could be used to show people what life in the early days was like and how the Historical Society had helped restore it.

"Jack McCracken is working at the mine now and he takes care of the cabin. When kids from Camp Galena hike to Morning Gulch, Jack will show them around.

"Lucy's dream has come true, and so has mine. I hope all of you will get a chance to see the gulch for yourself. Thank you." Jodi stepped off the stage to enthusiastic applause.

The director told the high schoolers that he'd like some students to help Jack McCracken tell the campers about Morning Gulch. "You could even wear period costumes," he said. "And Jodi has offered to tell the story in more detail to anyone who's interested. See me during the break if you want to volunteer."

"Good job, Jodi," Megan exclaimed when Jodi slipped into the seat beside her. As the students began to move around, she stood and stretched. "I think I'll volunteer to help your friend Jack. And then I have a dozen questions to ask you."

"What a story!" Peter said. "You should write a book!"

Then other kids surrounded Jodi. Megan watched. Suddenly being a counselor at school camp seemed much more than just a fun thing to do. Camp Galena held promise of real adventure.

egan threw her duffle bag into the van. "That's all of my stuff, Mom. What's holding up Peter?"

"I'm here." Peter clattered down the back steps and tossed his bag in beside Megan's. "Let's go." He climbed into the backseat and slid the door closed.

"It's barely daylight," Megan yawned. She settled back in the seat beside her mother. "I'm glad I left my hair long this fall. With it in braids, I'll look like a real pioneer when I tell the kids about Lucy Steincroft and her family, especially in that old-fashioned dress you made me—thanks, Mom."

"You're welcome." Sarah Lewis backed the van out of the driveway. "I wish I could see you in it at the cabin. Do you both have your cameras?"

"I've got mine."

"Me too," Peter said. "I'll get some good pics of your pioneer girl for you." Though Peter didn't turn 16 until next month, their parents had given him a camera as an early birthday gift. For the last couple of weeks, he'd been popping up when least expected, snapping pictures of Megan and the family.

"And I'll get some of you," Megan said to Peter. "I'm glad you went along with me to visit Jodi. It will be great for you to show the campers the old stable while

I'm telling others about the cabin."

A small school bus waited at Madrona High for the student counselors. The driver stood at the open emergency door, swinging sleeping bags and duffles into the back seats. He grabbed Megan's and Peter's and tossed them inside, then slammed the door. "All aboard for Camp Galena!"

As Megan climbed into the bus, she noticed Sean Bertram in the middle of a group. Her heart thumped as he glanced up. For a moment his eyes met hers, but he glanced away when someone spoke to him.

Peter sat with Jake. Only one person sat by herself— Willow Elizabeth Hanes. She seldom had to sit alone.

Megan indicated the seat beside her. "Okay if I sit here?"

Willow shrugged. "Go ahead."

Megan sat. "Wasn't the orientation day at Camp Galena fun?" she asked.

"I guess so," Willow answered in a grumpy voice.

"Is something wrong?" Megan asked. Willow had seemed to be having a great time at Saturday's orientation.

Willow slanted her green eyes toward the back of the bus. "That two-timing Sean! He promised he'd sit with me on the way to camp today!"

Megan glanced back. Girls sat on either side of Sean, but he was talking to the boys too. She wondered if Sean had walked right past Willow and the seat she had saved. How embarrassing!

"I'm sorry," she said.

"Doesn't matter," Willow said, with a toss of her silky mane. "He's not the only cute guy at camp. Did you see that good-looking recreation director?"

"Jeremy James? He's *old!*"

"So? He's still cute."

Jeremy *was* good looking, Megan thought. And very friendly. Something about him made her want to keep her distance, though.

Willow opened her fanny pack, drew out an emery board, and began to smooth one of her perfectly manicured fingernails. Megan stole a look at her own short, unpolished nails and stuck her hands in her jacket pockets.

Willow finished her repair and fixed curious green eyes on Megan. "What's this I heard you saying Saturday about wearing a costume at this place we're supposed to hike to ... Morning Gulch?"

"Well, remember Jodi Marsh? She spoke to us last week? She said that the old lady who lived there as a little girl donated some things to put in the cabin so it would look the same as it did when her family lived there. The director thought it would be nice for whoever tells the story to the campers to dress the part of a pioneer person. I said I'd do it."

"Oh," Willow said. She shifted restlessly and turned to talk to the people sitting behind them.

Obviously the thought of anything not centered on herself turned Willow glassy-eyed. But her lack of interest disturbed Megan only momentarily. When they arrived at the Chuckawamish River and Camp Galena, she'd meet the group of girls who'd be her special responsibility. She could hardly wait.

The sun had just risen above the peaks surrounding the Chuckawamish Valley when the school bus pulled into the camp's parking lot. A September blue sky promised a fine day, and sunlight shafting through tall trees turned the dew to steam wherever it touched the ground.

Mr. Davis, the bespectacled, middle-aged camp director, waited while the students spilled out of the bus and claimed their belongings.

"We're here!" Megan exclaimed. She and Peter grabbed their bags.

"We're here," Peter repeated. "I wonder if Willow still thinks I shouldn't be?"

Across the yard, Willow, while keeping an eye on Sean, chatted vivaciously with Jeremy James and a group of girls. Megan shrugged. "If you ask me, Willow thinks mostly about Willow. I wouldn't worry about her opinion."

Mr. Davis beckoned the student counselors and teachers to form a group. He welcomed them to Camp Galena, then repeated that each student counselor would be responsible to a teacher or other adult who would sleep in the cabins at night and teach the classes during the day. He gave out the cabin assignments and daily schedules.

"Megan Parnell and Willow Hanes, you will work with Miss Loring, who will be arriving with the campers shortly. Your cabin is Tamarack."

Oh, no! Share a cabin with Willow? Megan sent up a quick plea. Lord, You'll have to help me make the best of it! "See you later," she said to Peter and pushed forward to get the slip of paper with the names of her campers.

"Want to settle in before the kids get here?" Megan asked Willow.

Willow shrugged. "Might as well."

Megan slung her duffle bag over her shoulder and tucked her rolled-up sleeping bag under one arm. She walked beside Willow along a graveled path winding in and out of the trees and past other cabins.

"Wouldn't you know, we get the cabin that's farthest from everything," Willow complained.

"Yeah, but I love the cabins that are open in front, facing the river," Megan said. "We'll hear it rushing by all night long."

"What's to keep wild animals from coming in?"

"Nothing, I guess. But most wild animals are scared of people."

As they approached Tamarack, the path curved around the A-frame building to some steps and a deck. The fronts of both lower and upper floors were open, except for a low wall.

The cabin contained nothing more than a lot of metal bunks with thin mattresses and a broom leaning against the wall. Megan dropped her load on the floor and ran up the stairs that led to the loft. "It looks like one group of campers sleeps up here, the other downstairs. Which do you want?"

Willow climbed the steps high enough to peer into the loft. "I'll take upstairs," she said. "It's safer."

Megan ran back down the stairs. She unrolled her sleeping bag on the bunk nearest the front of the cabin and shoved her duffle under it. Nine bunks left. Her list of campers numbered eight, so the extra bunk must be for Miss Loring, the teacher. She picked up the broom and swept away a few stray leaves, then wandered down to the river.

When the fall rains began, Megan knew the Chuckawamish would run bank full and wild. Now shallow water rippled over cobbles and into a shady pool before flowing out of sight around a bend.

She lifted her eyes to the steep hillside opposite. A few cedar snags, silver in the sunlight, speared into the sky from the forested hill. What a beautiful spot!

"Dear Father," Megan whispered, "thank You for letting me come here. Help me be a friend to my campers and a good leader. And please, help me get along with Willow. In Jesus' name ..."

Shouts echoed through the woods. Megan hurried back to Tamarack. "The kids are here, Willow. Let's go meet them."

A short while later, Megan stood in the cabin, helping an assortment of sixth-grade girls turn it into home.

"How do you say your name?" she asked tall Tikela.

"Nobody ever gets it right," the girl said. "Say *Tea*kuhluh. Accent on the *Ti*."

Tikela's glossy black skin contrasted with the pale face and hair of skinny little Beth. Tammy, a stocky girl with fuzzy curls, laid claim to a corner bunk.

A girl named Kimberly set a second pair of expensive new sneakers beside the matching suitcases under her bed, hooked her thumbs in the waistband of her designer jeans, and looked around the cabin. "This is really primitive," she commented.

Pals Julie and Laurel took the bunks next to Miss

Loring's. Laurel unrolled her sleeping bag and scooted outside. Julie carefully laid out her own bag and pillow, then straightened Laurel's.

Laurel returned with a sturdy cardboard carton, which she set between their bunks. "I thought I remembered seeing this outside the mess hall." She pulled an extra towel out of her suitcase and draped it across the box. "See, a night table." She set her flashlight on top.

Megan sat down on her own bunk. The two girls next to it obviously were good friends. Soo Yun, small and quiet, grinned as Hanna Joy sang a campfire song off-key. Hanna Joy's blue eyes sparkled under the colorful bandanna cap she wore.

Megan wondered about the cap. Hanna Joy interrupted her song to ask, "Megan, what's black and white and red all over?"

"A newspaper?"

"No."

"An embarrassed zebra?"

"No." Hanna Joy opened her suitcase and pulled out a swimsuit, black with white polka dots. "It's me in my swimsuit when I get sunburned."

Megan laughed, picturing Hanna Joy in such a predicament.

"Hey, Megan, what do we do first?" someone called.

From the direction of the mess hall, a bell rang. She stood up. "Everyone ready? Let's go find out the day's schedule."

Back they all trooped, past other cabins, past the mess hall, to an amphitheater in the woods, where rows of rustic benches curved around a campfire circle and a

27

stage. Kids and student helpers hurried from all directions. Megan saw Peter bring in his group of boys. She and her campers found seats.

Mr. Davis, the director, explained the day's schedule. Then he introduced the teachers and student helpers. Megan stood with the other high school students when he called her name.

"Yea, Megan," cheered Hanna Joy. Megan grinned back at Hanna and her other campers.

"Okay," she said to the girls when they were dismissed. "First we do a river investigation with Miss Loring."

A couple of Megan's campers ran to hug Miss Loring. "Hi, Tikela, Tammy," she said, returning their hugs. She looked younger than the other teachers. She wore jeans, a sweatshirt, and folded-down rubber waders, and her hair hung in pigtails. She greeted Megan. "You're one of my student helpers? Good!"

Willow and her group joined them. "Listen, everybody." Miss Loring waited for attention. "We'll spend an hour or so at the river, then while I repeat the investigation with other groups, Megan and Willow will take you on a 'treasure-hunt' hike."

Megan checked her knapsack, making sure she had the booklets and papers from the orientation meeting. Remembering her prayer that morning and determined to be friendly to Willow, she moved closer to the other girl. "I'm glad we can work together."

"Are you?" Willow answered, staring across the amphitheater to where Sean and his campers were getting ready for their morning class. "I don't see why they can't put the boys and girls together for their classes."

Before Megan thought, the words popped out. "I wouldn't mind working with Sean either, but I guess we're stuck with each other." Too late, she clamped her lips together.

Willow's cheeks turned pink. She didn't answer.

Miss Loring picked up a bag of equipment and handed plastic dishpans and nets to some of the students to carry. Everybody followed her through the camp and down the riverbank to the beach in front of Tamarack cabin.

"We'll be talking a lot about how the river, the plants, and the wildlife depend on each other," said Miss Loring. "Even things we seldom notice, like tiny insects in the river, play a very important part in the life of the whole ecosystem."

One of the girls raised her hand. "What's an ecosystem?"

"I know, I know!" Hanna Joy bounced. "It's the living things that depend on each other, and their environment." She slapped at a mosquito on her arm. "Like that mosquito. She needed a meal of my blood so she could lay her eggs and make more mosquitos."

"That's right." The teacher laughed. "The Chuckawamish is a very important part of the ecosystem you see around us. It could be easily damaged by certain activities along its banks. One reason is that long ago, Ice Age glaciers dammed the rivers. The dammed-up rivers formed lakes, which eventually filled with sediments—sand or gravel or clay.

"When riverbanks like that are disturbed, by logging or farming or whatever, the sediments wash into the stream. If a lot of mud or clay gets into the water, it kills the insects. Then the fish have nothing to eat, and they disappear too."

Miss Loring picked up a mesh screen and a dishpan. "Let's find out how healthy this river is."

She chose Tikela and one of Willow's campers to take off their shoes and wade into the water to help her. Tikela held the pan while Miss Loring and the other student worked the flat mesh screen under some gravel then lifted it up so the water ran over the screen and into the pan.

"The mud on these rocks is slippery," the student commented as she picked her way back to the group.

Miss Loring frowned a little as she peered out where the river ran deeper. "That's probably just sediment washed down by the last rains," she said. "But the water does seem muddier than it should be for this time of year."

She set the pan down and turned to the girls. "Some of the insects that live near the river—stoneflies, caddis flies, mayflies—are what we call indicator species. Their babies, or larvae, need clean flowing water with a high oxygen content. They live in shallow riffles like these." She pointed to the rippling water. "If we find lots of their larvae, we know the river is healthy. Anyone here like to fish?"

Several girls raised their hands.

"Why do you think you would probably find fish in the quiet pool over there, below the riffle? Soo Yun?"

"Are they waiting for the water to wash insects down to them from the riffles?"

"Right." Miss Loring bent over the pan. "Okay, the mud's settling out. This water's pretty clear now."

The kids crowded around the dishpan. Megan could see a number of tiny creatures crawling and swimming in it.

"Ooh, gross!" Kimberly squealed.

Miss Loring took out some magnifiers with plastic containers that held a little water beneath the eyepieces. She put an insect or two into each container. The students peered through the eyepieces while she explained how to tell one kind of insect from another.

Megan picked a pebble out of the water's edge. She showed Miss Loring a small, dark green creature crawling over the wet stone.

"That's a caddis fly larva," the teacher said. "That kind spins a silk thread to anchor it to the rock. Other kinds of caddis flies collect bits of sand and gravel, or evergreen needles, and cement them around themselves to make traveling houses to hide in."

Megan dropped her find into one of the magnifiers. Under the eyepiece, her caddis fly larva became a monster with a body of green glass beads and a brown bead head with wicked-looking pincers. It grabbed a smaller, twin-tailed insect in its pincers. The small one twisted and fought back.

"Oh, look at this!" Megan cried. She handed the magnifier to Hanna Joy and Soo Yun.

"He's a meany!" Hanna Joy said.

31

Campers crowded to look. "I can't see," Tikela complained. She snatched the magnifier from Soo Yun. Her action was harder than she'd intended because the contents flew over her shoulder and splashed into Willow's face.

Willow yelped. Frantically she pawed droplets of water from her cheek and neck. "Are there bugs on me? Help me, somebody," she begged. Dancing about, she pulled her T-shirt away from her chest and shook it. She stumbled on the wet rocks and nearly fell.

Tikela watched this performance, open-mouthed. Some of the girls snickered.

"Willow!" Miss Loring said in a firm voice. "There are no bugs on you, and they wouldn't hurt you if there were." Plainly she meant that Willow should set a more dignified example.

Miss Loring gathered the campers around her and brought their attention back to the lesson, but Willow stalked a short distance away. Looking sulky, she bent her neck to let her long hair swing in front of her and shook it, section by section, then inspected her arms and even her legs.

"We've found several kinds of insects that need clear water and high oxygen levels," Miss Loring told the girls. "Would you say the river here is fairly healthy?"

"Yes," the girls chorused.

Another group of students appeared on the riverbank. "Willow and Megan will take you on your hike now," Miss Loring told the campers. "See you later."

Megan turned to Willow. "Shall we meet in front of Tamarack to give them their instructions?"

Willow shrugged. "Okay. I need to comb my hair anyway."

At the cabin, she disappeared up the stairs, leaving Megan to corral 16 lively girls. "That's not fair, Lord," Megan muttered under her breath. "I'm really going to need Your help to keep my mouth shut. My hair looks as bad as hers, but we're supposed to stay with these kids."

Camping Capers

"Listen, everybody!" Megan jumped up on the deck of the cabin and tried to get the girls' attention. "If you don't quiet down and listen we won't get back in time for lunch."

Hanna Joy and Soo Yun had been giggling together inside the cabin. They scampered out to join the other campers, Hanna Joy adjusting her red and white bandanna cap.

"In this treasure hunt," Megan said, "We're supposed to look for ways in which water affects our environment. Those ways are the treasures. The person who lists the most wins a prize."

"What's the prize?" somebody asked.

"Two prizes, actually. For one, no KP duty. For the other, the winner from each group gets to help Jeremy James, the recreation director, plan the evening campfire." Remembering the corny skits and songs from her own sixth-grade camping experience, Megan added, "That should be lots of fun."

Megan gave notebooks and pencils to her campers.

"Where's ours?" one of Willow's girls wanted to know. "Where's our counselor?"

"Willow, Willow, Willow," the girls chanted. Looking irritated, Willow ran down the stairs with notebooks and pencils.

"I didn't have time to read the information they gave us," she told Megan under her breath. "You'll have to be the leader."

"All right," Megan said. "But you have to help keep the group together."

She turned to the girls again. "I'll walk ahead. Willow will see that nobody gets left behind. We'll stop along the way so you can write your observations." She struck off through the camp and led them onto a level ridge that ran straight ahead through the forest. She stopped. "Who knows what we're standing on?" she asked.

"It looks like an old road," answered Hanna Joy.

"That's silly," argued Tikela. "It's too narrow for a road and there are trees growing in the middle of it."

"All guesses are allowed, Tikela," Megan said. "It *is* narrow, and there are trees growing on it, but Hanna Joy's very close. It's an old railroad bed. Over a hundred years ago a railroad ran along here, carrying ore from the mountain mines to the smelter in town."

She caught Tikela's scowl. Oh, dear, thought Megan. I didn't mean to make her mad, but I can't let her put others down.

"If it's a railroad," Tikela challenged, "where are the rails?"

"Well," Megan replied, "the river kept washing away the bridges and trestles. Finally the owners abandoned the railroad and took out the rails.

Soo Yun scribbled something in her notebook. "The river affects where road builders put roads. Is that good to list?"

"Sure." Megan turned to the others. "What else can you list?"

36

"The trees couldn't grow without water," one of the girls answered.

Soo Yun pointed to a swampy pool. "Water collects in low places and makes swamps."

"Are the plants and animals in a swamp different than in the river?" Megan asked.

Some of the girls squatted to peer into the pond. They jotted their observations. They all heard the plop as a frog leaped into the pool.

Willow leaned against a mossy tree trunk, looking bored.

"Anyone know why there is moss on that tree?" Megan asked.

"I know, I know," Hanna Joy bounced and waved her hand. "It's because there's so much rain here."

"Oh, you think you know everything!" Tikela exclaimed crossly, giving Hanna Joy's bandanna cap a yank. It slipped off her head.

Megan gasped. Without the cap, Hanna Joy's head shone round and white and hairless. Hanna Joy looked surprised. But not as surprised as Tikela. Tikela gasped too, and stared at the back of the other girl's head. Her frown disappeared as her face crinkled into an embarrassed smile.

Hanna Joy caught Soo Yun's eye and grinned as she turned to Tikela. The other girls looked shocked at what had happened, but suddenly a ripple of giggles ran through the group. Then they were all laughing because from the back of Hanna Joy's hairless head grinned a marking pen smiley-face, complete with blue eyes and freckles.

Hanna Joy laughed loudest of all at the joke she and Soo Yun had played.

"What happened to your hair?" Tikela asked.

"I have leukemia," Hanna Joy answered matter-of-factly. "The chemotherapy treatments made it fall out, but it will grow back. My leukemia is in remission."

"What's remission?" asked somebody else.

"The cancer symptoms are gone."

Megan wished someone had told her about Hanna Joy's illness. What if something should happen while she was in Megan's care? But Hanna Joy eased her worries. "The doctor says I can do anything I feel like doing." She replaced her bandanna cap. Her eyes twinkled mischievously. "And I feel like lunch. So let's get on with this hike."

"Do you think I should talk to Tikela about her attitude?" Megan whispered to Willow.

"I think Hanna Joy did more for Tikela's attitude than your talking to her could do," Willow answered, her eyes misty.

Surprised at Willow's reaction, Megan said, "You're probably right." As she led the group on along the old roadbed, she thought about the time she spent worrying about how her hair looked. "I'm sorry, Lord," she said softly. "I didn't know how blessed I am."

They came to the end of the marked trail and stopped so the girls could add more observations to their lists. Here the grade ended in a sudden drop to the river. Megan idly wondered why. Then she noticed some broken pilings sticking up from the curve of the river's edge. Must have been a trestle there.

On the far side of the river a stream flowed out of the woods and across a stony bank. Even from this distance, the stream looked muddy. The discoloration swirled into the clear Chuckawamish in a murky trail as the waters mixed and flowed downstream.

She caught a glimpse of movement across the river. A man stepped out of the woods and studied the stream. Then he turned and looked toward them. Megan felt a shock of recognition.

"Look." At her elbow, Hanna Joy pointed. "Isn't that Jeremy James? I wonder what he's doing."

At that moment, Jeremy saw them. He melted back into the brush so quickly Megan wondered if he'd really been there.

"I don't know what he's doing," she said to Hanna. "Mapping out a new hike, maybe."

After an outdoor lunch, the sixth-graders met with the teachers of their morning classes to review what they'd learned. Miss Loring waited at one of the tables. A group of boys who'd also done the river investigation joined the girls of Tamarack cabin there.

"Hi, Peter," Megan said, surprised. "I didn't know you did the same thing we did. Are you the only student counselor for your cabin?"

"No," Peter answered. "Sean Bertram's the other one. He's around here someplace."

"Really? You don't sound too thrilled," she commented.

"Oh, he's all right." He leaned over to stop a tussle between two of the boys. "We hiked along the old railroad grade while you were doing the river investigation."

Miss Loring clapped her hands for attention just as Sean came into the picnic area and slid onto a bench beside Willow. White teeth flashed as he grinned and whispered something in her ear. Willow fluttered her eyelashes. Megan felt a funny tightness in her throat. She forced herself to pay attention to the teacher, who was talking about the Chuckawamish watershed.

Then she realized someone was standing very close behind her. She twisted to see Jeremy James, his muscular arms folded, so near he almost leaned against her. Black eyes under bushy brows were fixed on Miss Loring as she spoke.

"Rain runs off the rocks or paving, or it soaks into the ground. It flows to the streams or rivers or lakes and finally to the ocean."

Megan shifted uncomfortably, wishing the brawny man behind her would step back. She turned again and said to him, "Did you have a nice hike this morning?"

A peculiar look crossed his face, and he stepped back. "What do you mean? I've been in camp all day."

"But I saw you across the river ..."

"You must be mistaken." Jeremy sauntered casually away to another table. Megan blinked. Why should he lie? But at least she'd made him go away.

"The rainfall carries more than just pure water," Miss Loring continued. "It can pick up pollutants from the air or from the ground. Remember that thin layer of mud we saw on the river rocks where the current is slow?" Many heads nodded. "Where did it come from?"

"Rain might have washed it into the river from the banks," someone answered. Megan thought of the muddy stream flowing into the Chuckawamish.

"That's why my dad is careful not to spill oil or gas on the ground when he works on his car," a boy said. "It could get into the water supply."

"That's right," said Miss Loring. She passed out diagrams of a watershed. They spent a few minutes discussing other pollutants that can get into the water system.

"Ugh," Kimberly said to the camper next to her. "I'm going to have my parents buy bottled water from now on."

The teacher told the students to put the diagrams in their notebooks. "Now comes the moment you've been waiting for." She smiled. "Counselors, collect the papers from this morning's treasure hunt. Look through them and bring me the longest lists. Jeremy James is going to help me pick the winners."

As Megan collected the lists from her campers, Jeremy drifted back to joke with her girls. She began to scan the papers. Suddenly she felt his hand on her shoulder.

"Aren't you the young lady who's going to tell us about Morning Gulch tomorrow?" Jeremy James grinned, his eyes friendly and interested. Megan felt disoriented. He'd just told her a barefaced lie. Now he acted as if nothing at all had happened.

"Oh ... yes." She stammered. "I'll do my best, anyway."

"Good. We'll be working together." His hand remained on her shoulder a little too long for a casual touch. Megan hopped up and moved to the end of the table to escape that warm and heavy hand. She spread out the papers, feeling a little silly that such a thing should bother her. She picked up two papers, Laurel's and Soo Yun's, and handed them to Jeremy. "Here. These are the two longest lists."

He compared the lists and gave Laurel's back to Megan. "Who's Soo Yun? She has the most."

Soo Yun raised her hand with a shy smile while Hanna Joy squeezed her friend. "You won! No KP and you get to work with Jeremy!"

Soo Yun and the other winners were called to the front for applause. Then they went off with Jeremy to plan the evening's program while Miss Loring dismissed the rest of the campers for classes of their choice.

Megan helped students from the crafts class collect and identify leaves from different trees in the camp. Then they made leaf prints with ink and rollers. After that she joined another group for a lesson about the kinds of rocks found in the riverbed.

Then it was recreation time. The Tamarack cabin girls were paired with Peter's and Sean's boys for a game of softball.

"Do we have to play against the boys?" complained Kimberly.

"Yeah," Tikela agreed. "That's not fair."

"I know what we can do," Megan told them. "Half of the boys and half of the girls can play on each team."

"Good idea," said Jeremy James, jogging up to them. "Sean, your group and Megan's will be one team. Peter's and Willow's groups will be the other."

Willow, who'd headed over to talk to Sean as the kids collected on the ball field, made a disgusted face.

"Choose your captains and a name for your team,"

Jeremy instructed them.

Peter's and Willow's team named themselves the "Buzzers." Megan's and Sean's campers picked the "Bombers."

The Buzzers won the toss for the first turn at bat, and the Bombers ran out on the field—all except Soo Yun, who tapped Megan's arm.

"I don't want to play, Megan." Her previously cheerful face looked pale and pinched.

"Don't you feel well, Soo Yun?"

"I just don't want to play. Can I go back to the cabin?"

"Why don't you sit and watch?"

"All right." Head drooping, Soo Yun sat down with her back against a tree trunk.

One of the Buzzers connected with the ball and dashed to first base. The second batter walked and so did the third. Far out in left field, Tikela caught the fourth batter's fly ball. "You're out!" called Jeremy James from the umpire's spot, and Megan forgot about Soo Yun in the excitement of the game.

"How do you like counseling so far?" Sean asked her while they waited for the next batter up.

"Great," she answered. "How's it going for you?"

"All right. Spending three days with a bunch of middle-schoolers isn't my idea of a really good time, but these volunteer things look great when school elections come around. And they can't hurt on my college application either."

"College application!" Megan exclaimed. "You're thinking about college already?"

"Can't start too early if you want to make the best schools."

"Oh." She'd never met anyone quite like Sean. He seemed so ... so in control.

Near the backstop, she noticed Peter examining something on the ground. Willow leaned against the backstop, staring at Sean and Megan. She started toward them just as Peter straightened up with something in his hand. He called her name and stretched his hand out to show her.

Willow craned her neck to look. With a screech that cut through the yells of the kids on the ball field, she jumped back, then turned and ran toward Sean and Megan. With a look of mischief, Peter followed her.

"Keep it away, oh, keep it away!" Willow shrieked, grabbing Sean's arm and whirling around behind him.

"What's the matter?" Sean asked.

"It's just a caterpillar." Peter opened his hand to show them the biggest, greenest caterpillar Megan had ever seen.

"Oh, Peter. It's pretty!" Megan exclaimed. Big as her finger, it was smooth and a lovely pale green with a curving horn at either end. Even as she spoke, she caught Sean's look of disbelief. Oops! she thought. I guess he expects all girls to be scared of insects.

Sean turned to the quaking Willow. "It won't hurt you," he said soothingly, patting the hand still clutching his arm. To Peter he said in a scornful voice, "Why don't you grow up?"

"Strike three! You're out," yelled the umpire. The Bombers rushed in from the field. The Buzzers ran out to take their places.

Peter clamped his lips tight and walked away.

Megan hurried after him. "I don't think Sean meant that the way it sounded," she told him, feeling vaguely disloyal to Peter. "You really shouldn't have chased Willow with it."

He returned the caterpillar to the ground behind the backstop. It began to burrow its way into the soft earth. "Sean meant it," he said. "And I wasn't going to chase Willow, until she screamed. If you ask me, they're both a couple of fakes."

All the campers crowded into the lantern-lit amphitheater for the evening campfire. Those who had worked on the program with Jeremy James hung a sheet in front of the stage then dragged a table behind the sheet. Megan spotted Soo Yun standing apart from the other contest winners.

"Hi!" Hanna Joy plopped down next to Megan.

"Hi. How did you like the first day of camp?" Megan asked her.

"I had a wonderful time." Hanna Joy drew out the word *wonderful*. Then her face sobered as she looked toward the group around Jeremy James. "I don't know what's the matter with Soo Yun, though. She's acted really strange all afternoon."

"Maybe she's homesick."

"Maybe."

Mr. Davis, the camp director, stepped in front of the sheet. First he explained about the daily Clean Cabin Contest. Then he announced, "Tomorrow you have your choice of two field trips. One trip will include tours of the ranger station, a fish farm, and a fish ladder. The other choice is a hike to an old mine at Morning Gulch and the cabin where the miner's family lived."

Peter scooted in on Megan's other side. "I wonder how many will want to go to Morning Gulch," he whispered.

47

"I don't know," she whispered back, looking around at the crowd of sixth-graders. "Even half of this bunch would be quite a lot to keep track of."

The buzz around them quieted as Jeremy James, wearing a long cape and an old-fashioned top hat, stepped onto the stage. "Ladies and gentlemen," he proclaimed with a sweeping bow, "the Camp Galena Thespian Society presents an evening of dramatic entertainment. First on the program, let me introduce Dr. Sew-em-up in 'The Operation.' "

A bright light glowed from behind the sheet, throwing the table's shadow onto the makeshift screen. On the table lay the "patient." Dr. Sew-em-up and his assistant, also in silhouette, argued over the patient's illness. They decided to operate.

"I'm sure it's appendicitis," said the doctor, lowering a saw and appearing to cut into the patient.

"Oh no, sir," his assistant replied. "I'm sure it's a cancer." His shadow chopped away with a hatchet in the vicinity of the patient's abdomen.

The doctor put down his saw and took up a huge knife, then a hammer. His assistant brought out a big pair of scissors. Finally the doctor pulled out what looked like yards and yards of rope. "See," he said, "it *is* appendicitis."

The assistant reached in and pulled out a can. "No, see? It's a can, sir."

It took a moment for the students to catch the joke, then they laughed and clapped.

After more skits, Jeremy James led them in singing camp songs. Finally they were all dismissed to walk through the dark woods to their cabins. Megan and Willow, carrying flashlights, walked down the path to Tamarack together.

"Are you going to Morning Gulch tomorrow?" Megan asked.

"No. I'm not much for hiking," Willow yawned. "Besides, Sean's going on the other trip."

Megan felt a prick of irritation. Knowing Willow, she'd make the most of her opportunity to be near Sean.

Miss Loring had reached the cabin before them. She hung a battery powered lantern on the wall then went to the loft to help Willow settle her girls for the night. The campers giggled and chatted as they pulled night-clothes out of duffles. Megan urged them to get in bed and quiet down. "Tomorrow's going to be even busier than today," she told them. "Remember, we want to be up in time to get ready for the Clean Cabin Contest."

"Who's going to pick the winning cabin?" someone called.

"Jeremy James," said Kimberly. "I heard him talking to one of the teachers."

"I like him!" said Laurel.

In the cot beside Megan, Soo Yun turned over and buried her face in the pillow. Hanna Joy gave her friend a worried look.

"Well, Megan," said Miss Loring, coming down the stairs. "Everybody in their sleeping bags?"

"Everybody but me," said Megan, unzipping her bag and tumbling in. She thrust her feet to the bottom and quickly drew them up again as Tikela muffled a giggle. Reaching down, she felt around for the prickly spruce cones the jokester had put in her sleeping bag. She tossed them over the half-wall beside her bed. Miss Loring switched off the lantern. Megan lay there in the peaceful darkness as the girls' whispers died away, listening to the *shush-shush* of the river.

She was nearly asleep when the crack of a breaking branch roused her. She heard a rustle of leaves, as if some animal moved near the cabin. She heard it again, farther away, and smiled, remembering Willow's remark about being safer on the second floor.

Sometime later that night, Megan opened her eyes. Between black branches silhouetted against blacker sky, stars twinkled like the lights of faraway cities. For a moment she couldn't remember where she was. Then the sound that had wakened her came again, close by, but muffled by blankets.

Quietly she slipped out of bed and knelt beside Soo Yun's bunk. "Soo Yun," she whispered, "why are you crying?" The girl's shoulder stiffened under her hand as Soo Yun tried to choke back her sobs. "Do you hurt someplace?"

In the darkness she felt Soo Yun shake her head.

"Are you homesick?"

Again Soo Yun shook her head.

"I'd like to help." Megan took her hand. "Can't you tell me what's wrong?"

"It's nothing," Soo Yun whispered. "I'm sorry I woke you."

"I'll sit here 'til you go to sleep, okay?" Megan pulled her sleeping bag to the floor and sat in it with the open end around her shoulders. She held Soo Yun's hand until she was sure the girl was sleeping then grog-gily crawled onto her own bed.

"Heavenly Father," she whispered as she sank toward sleep, "I don't know what's wrong with Soo Yun, but You do. Please show me how to help her."

Much too early in the morning the ringing of the mess hall bell woke the campers. Megan groaned.

Miss Loring sat on her bunk, dressed and braiding her hair.

"Good morning, Megan," she said. "I have to meet with the rest of the teachers before breakfast. Remember, Clean Cabin check starts in half an hour!" She cinched the end of each braid with a rubber band, climbed the steps to give the same message to Willow, then left.

In minutes the cabin jiggled with activity. Girls ran back and forth to the restrooms, tried on and rejected outfits, smoothed and re-smoothed sleeping bags. Morning people shouted and sang; night owls grum-bled. Hanna Joy bubbled, but Soo Yun looked tired and said very little.

After last night's interrupted sleep, Megan sympa-thized with the grumblers. She could hear Willow upstairs, sounding bright and cheery, urging her girls to hurry.

Tikela grabbed the broom and swept around and under her bunk. She handed the broom to the next girl and began to repack her suitcase.

Laurel flew out of the cabin to look for pretty leaves for her cardboard box dressing table. Julie straightened Laurel's sleeping bag.

Megan yawned at herself in her hand mirror. "My

hair looks like a bird's nest," she grumbled, then shut her mouth as she noticed Hanna Joy pulling a clean bandanna cap over her head, one that matched her pink polo shirt. Megan swept a brush through her tangled curls, tossed brush and mirror into her duffle, and tucked it under her bed.

"Give me the broom." Tikela took it as Soo Yun finished. "I'll do your section and the deck, Megan."

"Thanks," Megan said.

"Here comes Jeremy," Tikela called a few minutes later. She stood the broom in its place.

"Everybody out!" Jeremy called. "Time for Clean Cabin check."

The girls swarmed past Jeremy as he mounted the steps. "Jeremy, be sure to look at my autumn bouquet," Laurel pleaded.

"You won't find a speck of dirt anywhere upstairs," bragged one of Willow's campers.

Jeremy bantered with the girls, tugging a ponytail here, squeezing a shoulder there.

Instead of joining the banter, Soo Yun stayed so close to Megan as they went down the steps that Megan nearly tripped over her. Something's wrong, she reminded the Lord. Please help.

Clean Cabin awards would be given at breakfast. Most of the campers started for the mess hall to await the breakfast bell, but Megan noticed that Soo Yun and Hanna Joy slipped away toward the river. She followed, stopping at the edge of the trees to watch them make their way to a big rock near the water and sit down.

Megan turned in the other direction to walk along

52

the damp sand at the river's edge. Someone else had recently walked this way. A man, from the size and shape of the footprints. A bit of trash caught her eye, and she stooped to pick it up. It was a yellow cardboard box, like film canisters come in. Maybe one of the teachers had been out taking early morning photographs. She glanced at the box. ASA speed 3500? He must have been taking pictures very early ... maybe even in the dark! She flattened the box and stuck it in her pocket to throw away later. A few steps farther on she found a log to sit on. She watched the sun touch the silver snags on the hilltop across the river. Soon it would spill over the dark evergreens and down the hill.

"Lord," she prayed, "keep all of us safe on the hike to Morning Gulch. Help Peter and me make the story of the Steincroft family real to the campers. Help me show the kids how important You were to Lucy and her family.

"And, heavenly Father, please help me to get along with Willow. If You don't mind my asking, I'd like to get to know Sean much better. And please, Lord, don't forget Soo Yun."

The breakfast bell sounded. Megan saw Hanna Joy and Soo Yun coming along the river bank toward her. She went to meet them.

Soo Yun had been crying again. Hanna Joy looked scared but determined.

"Megan," Hanna Joy called. "Soo Yun needs to tell you something. Can we talk to you? Now?"

Megan's stomach rumbled, but breakfast would have to wait. "Of course," she said. "Where?"

Hanna Joy glanced up the path toward the cabin.

"Back there, where you were sitting. Not here."

"Okay." Megan led the way back to her log. "Now, what's this about?"

Hanna Joy looked at her friend, then back at Megan. "If someone touches you in a way that makes you uncomfortable, you should tell someone. Right?"

"Right," said Megan, a feeling of apprehension growing inside her.

"Well, someone touched Soo Yun that way, and now she's afraid to be around that person anymore. She wants to go home."

Megan's anger flared at that unknown person. Her heart twisted with sympathy as Soo Yun stared at her feet. She groped for words.

"I ... I don't know what to say, Soo Yun." She paused. "People who do things like that are sick. What happened?"

Soo Yun threw Megan a despairing look from under downcast lashes. She shuddered. "First he just wanted to take pictures of me ... for a camp scrapbook, he said. Then he said he'd teach me a game. He tried to get me to take my clothes off, and then he started putting his hands ... where ... where he shouldn't. He scared me, Megan. He made me feel so ashamed."

"How awful! What did you do?"

"I pulled away and ran. But he caught up before I got to camp. He grabbed my arms and put his face close to mine." Soo Yun shuddered again. "He said ... he said if I told anyone, he'd say I was lying and they'd send me home from camp. Megan, I can't let that happen. My parents would be disgraced!"

"But it wasn't your fault! Was it a camper or someone who works here?"

Soo Yun hung her head again. A tear ran down one cheek.

"You don't have to tell me. But you need to tell one of the grown-ups. He might bother other kids if you don't."

"He's a friend of all the grown-ups. No one would believe me against him," Soo Yun said bitterly.

"I believe you," Megan said.

"Soo Yun, if you don't tell," Hanna Joy said, "I will."

A footstep behind them made them jump. "Tell what?"

"Miss Loring!" said Megan. "Why aren't you at breakfast?"

"Because you girls weren't there. Since I'm responsible for you, I came looking. Care to tell me what's wrong?"

Megan let out her breath in a sigh of relief. Soo Yun's problem was too big for her to solve alone.

Miss Loring listened to the story without comment, reassuring Soo Yun, as Megan had, that none of it was her fault.

"He asked me to come out in the woods to help him find some sticks to use for a skit. Then he said he'd teach me a game ..." She broke down in sobs.

"Who was this person, Soo Yun?"

Soo Yun looked up at Miss Loring, then dropped her eyes.

She whispered, "Jeremy James."

"Jeremy James? Oh, that can't be ... his dad's a well-known doctor, and Jeremy loves to work with kids. His college major is in parks and recreation. The kids all like him ..."

Soo Yun flashed Megan a look that said, *See? What did I tell you about grown-ups?*

Miss Loring caught the look. "Oh, Soo Yun, I believe you. I'm just shocked. I'd never have suspected ..."

"Well," Megan said, "I would. He's made *me* uncomfortable. And Soo Yun has not been herself ever since yesterday morning when she and the other winners of that contest met with him."

Miss Loring thought a moment. "All right," she said. "For now, you girls must have your breakfast. Soo Yun, Jeremy James will not bother you or any other child again if I can help it."

By the time they reached the mess hall, most of the campers had finished eating. Miss Loring went in with Megan and the two girls and asked the cook to be sure they got something to eat. Then she disappeared.

While they were eating, Peter stuck his head into the room.

"Hey, Megan! Tamarack almost got the Clean Cabin Award. Better luck tomorrow."

"Who got it?" Hanna Joy asked.

"Fireweed," Peter told her. "You lost out to a bunch of boys!" He turned back to Megan. "I just saw the lists of who's going on each field trip. The kids are pretty evenly divided."

Soo Yun's story had so shaken Megan that she'd forgotten the Morning Gulch hike. It took a moment to realize what Peter was talking about. "Oh ... oh, that's good," she said absently for another thought had struck her.

Half of the student counselors and teachers would

be going on the hike too, but as recreation director, Jeremy James was supposed to oversee the organization of this outing. And as hostess at the Steincroft cabin, she would have to work closely with him. She put down her fork, her stomach suddenly in knots.

"You're not getting sick, are you, Megan?" Peter asked. "Your face looks funny." He searched for a better word. "I mean, you look sort of white."

"I'm all right." She glanced at the girls, neither of whom had eaten much.

"Hanna Joy, Soo Yun ... if you're through eating, you'd better run to class now. They'll talk about some of the things you'll be seeing on the field trips."

"All right." Hanna Joy slid off the bench and hugged Megan. "Thanks for helping."

Megan returned the hug. "Thank *you!* You're a good friend to have, Hanna Joy." She hugged Soo Yun too. "Now don't worry," she whispered to her. "It's going to be all right."

Peter watched the girls leave. "What was that all about?"

"I can't tell you now, Peter. But please, pray with me that the hike will go okay."

Peter looked puzzled, but he nodded. "Sure. That girl in the bandanna has cancer, doesn't she? Is she going on the hike?"

"She's planning on it."

"Aren't you afraid she might get sick?"

Megan worried too, but she repeated Hanna Joy's words. "The doctor says she can do anything she feels like doing."

The two walked down the steps together. "Did you see

57

all the sack lunches in the kitchen?" he asked.

"I didn't notice," Megan replied. "But I heard that the kids will eat their lunches outside the cabin while we're talking to small groups. Then everyone will go on to the mine together."

"Sounds good," said Peter. "I wonder where Jeremy James is. Weren't you supposed to meet with him after breakfast to go over the plans?"

Megan's stomach tightened again. She didn't want to work with Jeremy James or even be near him. Lord, she prayed silently, You know how I've looked forward to this day. I asked You to come with us and make it a good day. How can You possibly make good come out of what's happened?

"There's Jeremy now," said Peter. "And Miss Loring and Mr. Davis."

Jeremy James strode out of the building where he and other non-counseling staffers stayed. He flung a bulging duffle bag over his shoulder. As he came down the steps, his black brows were drawn together in a ferocious scowl. The other adults watched as he slammed the bag into his sports car parked nearby.

"What's going on?" Peter wondered. "They all look upset."

"They are," Megan said. "But I'm not sure what's going on."

Jeremy stormed back into the building, returned with another load of belongings, and tossed them into the car. Gravel spurted and the engine roared as car and driver careened out of the camp.

Mr. Davis saw the two of them and called, "Megan,

may we talk to you? Peter, you too."

"Are we in trouble?" Peter whispered to Megan.

"Not us. Jeremy is," she whispered back. "But this isn't going to be fun."

M r. Davis ushered Megan, Peter, and Miss Loring into the room he used as camp office. His tanned face looked solemn. "Megan, does Peter know what happened?"

She shook her head.

Briefly, Mr. Davis sketched out the accusation against Jeremy James. "He denied everything," the camp director said. "But we've notified the police. Until we clear the matter up, Mr. James is suspended from his job."

"Meanwhile, we must continue the camp program. We can spare one of the more mature student counselors from the other field trip. That person can go along on the hike and take care of some of Jeremy's responsibilities."

Good, thought Megan. One problem solved.

Mr. Davis continued. "You two will go ahead with your part as planned."

"What about Soo Yun?" asked Megan. "She wants to go home."

"I'd like to see her stay at camp, but we'll do whatever's best for her. I've phoned her parents, and they want to think it through and call me back and talk to Soo Yun. Does anyone else know about this?"

"Only Hanna Joy and me," answered Megan. "And Miss Loring and now, Peter."

61

"Since Jeremy is gone, no one else needs to know right now. We'll just tell the campers he had to leave ... which is true." Mr. Davis paused and brushed his graying hair off his forehead. "Megan, Peter, it makes me more angry than I can say that things like this happen. I'm sorry you have to be involved."

A whoop from the woods and campers bursting into the clearing announced that the morning class was over. Peter headed toward his cabin to get his campers ready for the field trips.

"Don't forget to bring your camera," Megan called after him.

"Do you think you and Willow can get the Tamarack girls organized?" Miss Loring asked as she and Megan walked together toward their cabin. "I'd like to spend some time with Soo Yun."

"Yes," said Megan. The campers were in the cabin, full of questions about what they should take. Megan quickly checked her knapsack into which she'd already packed the long-skirted calico dress and matching sunbonnet. "I hope I can remember all of the story I'm supposed to tell," she whispered to herself. No room to carry shoes. She'd have to wear her hiking boots with the outfit. She sat on her bunk to put them on while answering questions.

Hanna Joy came in alone. "Soo Yun's with Miss Loring and the camp nurse," she told Megan quietly. "I don't think she's going to go with us."

"Are you sure *you* feel up to going, Hanna Joy?"

"I don't like to leave my friend. But I haven't been hiking since before I got sick. I really want to go."

Megan made sure her campers had everything they needed, then sent them to the buses. She went upstairs to check with Willow.

Willow's girls weren't ready. She sat applying makeup. "A whole day with Sean," she purred. "I've got to look my best."

"I hope the makeup helps," snapped Megan. To Willow's campers she said, "The buses are loading. Who's going on the hike?" Several girls bounced up to her. "You have to wear boots or sturdy shoes," she told a girl with sandals on her bare feet.

The girl hurried to put on socks and shoes. Megan told another girl to change from shorts to jeans.

Finally she herded the last one out of the cabin and stalked after them. Willow caught up with her on the trail. "Don't be jealous, Megan," she said. "After all, Sean could have chosen to go on the hike."

Jealous! Megan stifled a tart reply. Willow was not only lazy and vain, she was impossible!

In the parking lot, Sean was passing out lunches. He handed one to Willow, who smiled sweetly and fluttered her eyelashes.

"Want to sit with me on the bus, Sean?"

"Thanks," said Sean, handing a brown paper bag to Megan. "But I won't be going on the fisheries tour after all. Mr. Davis asked if I'd fill in for Jeremy James on the Morning Gulch hike."

Suddenly, the gloomy cloud that had surrounded Megan all morning evaporated. No Jeremy James. Sean Bertram instead! And to make the moment more delicious, Willow stood with her lipsticked mouth hanging open, speechless.

A few minutes later, Willow's bus pulled away. In the other bus, campers made faces and waved at Peter, who stood next to the driver, trying to angle his camera to get everyone into his photo. Megan peered out the window anxiously. Where was Miss Loring?

Oh, there she came from the direction of the nurse's cabin. She stopped briefly in the clearing to speak to Mr. Davis, then hopped aboard. "Everybody here?"

From the back of the bus where he'd been checking the list of campers going on the hike, Sean called, "All here."

The bus engine growled and turned over. The driver shifted into low gear. They moved ahead a few feet, then the engine coughed and died. In the overhead mirror Megan saw the puzzled expression on the driver's face as he tried again to start the engine. Then his gaze dropped to the gauges on the instrument panel and puzzlement turned to disbelief.

"Out of gas!" he muttered. "I filled the tank before we left town. It can't be out of gas." He jerked open the door and jumped out. Megan craned her neck. She saw him strip a slender wand from a nearby bush. He did something at the back of the bus—checked the level of fuel in the tank, she guessed.

He reappeared in the doorway of the bus. "Sorry, everybody. We *are* out of gas."

A groan went up from the campers. Miss Loring tried to shush them. "Isn't there extra here at camp?"

"Not that I know of," the driver said. "Could have siphoned some from the other bus, but it's too late for that now."

"Can't we borrow some from one of the staffers' cars?" a boy near the front asked.

The driver shook his head. "Wouldn't be enough. A bus takes a lot of gas. The trail's not far, but we've got to go all the way back to Madrona Bay tomorrow."

"It would take a long time to get some from town." Mr. Edgebert, one of the teachers, stood. "How about if all the kids meet over by the mess hall? Some of you counselors organize some games while we decide what we do next." He designated Sean and a couple of the other high schoolers to be in charge.

Disappointed, the kids filed off the bus. Megan stood for a moment, watching as the bus driver slid under the bus to check the underside of the gas tank. The pebbles of the parking area looked clean and dry. If the gas had leaked out, wouldn't there be a stain?

She saw Mr. Davis across the yard speaking with the teachers. Peter appeared at her side.

"Something's funny here," he said in a low voice.

"What do you mean?"

Peter took her elbow and steered her away from the adults. "Well, it might not mean anything at all ... but last night, after everybody was asleep, one of my boys got sick to his stomach. I took him to the nurse's cottage ... had to wake her up, then stayed with my camper for a while. He's okay, but she decided he'd better sleep in the infirmary so she could keep an eye on him. It was pretty late when I started back to my cabin."

"So?" Megan stopped walking and looked into Peter's serious blue eyes.

"So I nearly jumped out of my skin when I met Jeremy James on the path in the dark. He didn't have a light, and mine was pretty dim. He seemed to come out of nowhere, over near the storage shed back there." Peter pointed into the woods, behind the bus, where part of a roof showed through the branches.

"So?" Megan repeated.

"So I think I scared him too. He didn't ask what I was doing out that late or anything, like you'd expect."

"Did he say *anything?*"

"He said, 'Got to get this stuff back to my room,' and pushed past me. He was carrying something bulky. I thought it was a suitcase—things he'd used at the campfire. But that late?"

Megan opened her mouth to say that Jeremy could have come that way to get to the staff's quarters, but Peter wasn't through. "The strangest thing though, didn't hit me until just now."

"What's that?"

"The smell of gas. As he went past, I smelled gasoline."

"You think he took it?" Megan paused. "What would he possibly want with so much gasoline? Even if he was stealing it for his car, he wouldn't empty the whole gas tank."

"And if it was for his car, he wouldn't have been back there in the woods," Peter said. "I think we'd better tell somebody."

The two of them walked back to where Mr. Davis, the teachers, and the bus driver were discussing the situation.

"Mr. Davis, could we talk to you?" Peter asked.

The camp director excused himself and turned to Peter, who told him what he'd just told Megan.

"It doesn't make sense," Mr. Davis said. "And unfortunately, we can't check with Mr. James at the moment. But we can go take a look around." He led them across the parking area and into the woods near the storage building. They circled the shed but saw nothing unusual. Mr. Davis tried the knob. The door swung inward. "Unlocked," he said. "That's odd."

Inside, shovels and rakes and lawn trimmers and rolled-up hoses hung from the walls. Shelves held cans with dried paint dribbled down their sides, bottles of mysterious liquids, small tools, and boxes. Chairs and benches waiting for repair were stacked in the back. In front of these sat a rusty lawn mower. There was also a jumble of wooden crates and metal containers, scattered as though someone had rummaged through them.

Mr. Davis hefted a metal five-gallon can and set it down again. He unscrewed the lid and sniffed. "Gasoline."

"This one's full too," Peter said, lifting and shaking it. "And here's another."

"Good thing you set us on to this," Mr. Davis said, nudging an open bucket of gasoline with his toe. "I don't know what he was planning, but leaving gas in an open container like this is an invitation to disaster."

"Can we put the gas back in the bus?" Megan asked.

Mr. Davis thought. "I guess no law was broken. We wouldn't be disturbing evidence." He picked up a length of rubber tubing and sniffed it. "Here's what he used to siphon the gas from the tank. Do we have a funnel of some kind on those shelves over there?"

Peter found a large one, which he handed to Megan. He and Mr. Davis each picked up a container of gasoline. They all returned to the bus. The astonished driver poured the fuel through the funnel and into the gas tank. When all of the gasoline in the shed had been returned to the tank, Mr. Davis sent word to the campers to use the bathrooms, get drinks, and then return to their seats on the bus.

This time the engine started perfectly. They drove up the valley then turned onto a gravel road. Megan watched for the trail as the bus lumbered along, still puzzling over Jeremy James' odd behavior. He hadn't known last night he'd be fired this morning. Why would he want to sabotage the bus?

Peter turned around in his seat. He pointed to a slash that led into the forest. "Look!" he exclaimed. "A new road. Do you suppose it goes to Morning Gulch?"

"Jodi didn't mention a road." Megan noted the newly laid crushed rock. "Maybe the Forest Service is building it."

The bus lumbered on for a few hundred yards then stopped at a small, arrow-shaped sign with the words *Morning Gulch*. At last! In spite of Jeremy James, they would soon see Lucy Steincroft's cabin and meet Jack McCracken and see the gold mine Jodi and the boys had discovered.

Miss Loring stood up and asked for attention. "Students, we have three objectives for this hike ... to learn about mining, to learn how the pioneers lived in these forests and mountains, and to learn all we can about the ecosystem here.

"Most of all, we want you to enjoy yourselves. Remember the rules we've discussed for safe hiking. If you think you are getting blisters on your feet, see Sean Bertram. He has the first aid kit.

"Leave what you see as you find it so people who come after us will have an enjoyable experience too."

Megan and Peter got off the bus first and led the students toward the trail. "Wait for me, Megan." Hanna Joy caught up with them. "Can I hike with you?"

"Sure," Megan answered.

They crossed over a streamlet on a new plank bridge and followed the winding trail uphill between giant cedar and fir trees. In places where the sun penetrated, huckleberry brush and sword fern splashed green against the brown forest floor.

Megan looked back at the long line of campers and counselors. Not far behind her, Miss Loring had stopped to point out a scrubby little evergreen growing in the shade of the bigger trees. She and Hanna Joy walked back so they could hear better.

"This is a yew tree," the teacher told the group around her. "It doesn't get very big, and it grows widely scattered throughout the forest. For years, people thought it was worth nothing, although its wood makes beautiful strong bows for archery. Loggers didn't bother to salvage it." She pointed out the dark, shiny needles growing in flat rows on either side of a twig. "But scientists have found a very important use for the yew tree. Does anyone know what that might be?"

She waited.

"I know," Hanna Joy called. "They make a cancer drug out of its bark."

"That's right," said Miss Loring. "It doesn't fight all cancers, but it does help at least one kind that couldn't be helped before."

"Does it help leukemia, Hanna Joy?" Megan asked.

"No. But who knows?" she gestured to the masses of foliage around them. "Maybe someday one of these other plants might be used to treat people with leukemia."

The three went on, followed by the first cluster of campers, while Miss Loring pointed out the yew tree to another group.

Over the voices of the hikers, Megan heard a distant rumble. "Must be on that road we passed before we got to the trail," she told Peter. "I wonder what it is."

"Don't know," he said.

Though they listened, they didn't hear the sound again. After a time they came to an overgrown rock slide. Jodi Marsh had told of struggling to find the trail here on her first trip to Morning Gulch. In the open, the sun shone hot on their heads. Big grasshoppers whirred from the rocks as they passed.

"The trail is easier now," she told Hanna Joy as they labored up the switchbacks. "The first time Jodi came, she and the boys had to push through the brush."

"Slow down, Megan," Peter said. "I want to get a picture of everybody coming up the switchbacks."

He puffed ahead. As he stood above them on a fallen log, aiming his camera down at the line of hikers, Megan snapped a quick picture of him with her own camera.

Someone yelled, "When can we stop and rest?"

"As soon as we get to the trees up there," she called back. Hanna Joy stumbled and Megan reached to steady her. "How are you doing, Hanna Joy?"

"I'll make it," she panted.

When Megan reached the top of the clearing, she looked back for Sean. She saw him midway in the line, laughing with one of the other girl counselors. They seemed to be having a fine time, Megan noted ruefully.

As they reached the shade of the trees, everyone flopped down to rest. Most of the hikers dug into their lunches for the trail mix the cooks had included. "Don't drink too much of your water," Megan cautioned them. "We've still got a long way to go."

"This is beautiful," Miss Loring said, indicating the valley below and the mountain peaks beyond. "These big old trees! Just think, some of them were here when Columbus came to America."

Mr. Edgebert, a little man wearing a baseball cap over his thinning hair, nodded. "Wasn't it near here where that seabird was discovered? The one that spends most of its time at sea but nests inland?"

"Oh, the marbled murrelet," Miss Loring answered. "You're right. Researchers did find nests in some old-growth hemlock trees someplace near here."

Peter propped himself against the log Megan perched on and offered her a stick of gum. "We must be fifty miles from salt water," he said. "That's a long way for seabirds to fly."

"We can ask our guest speaker when she comes to show slides at the campfire tonight," Miss Loring said.

"She's a bird expert."

Megan stared out across the valley. Several large brown patches where the trees had been cut recently scarred the hillsides. Other patches, logged years ago, were now the uniform green of trees all one size, all one kind. No complex ecosystem there. No place for yew trees or marbled murrelets or all the marvelous variety of plants and animals God had created to depend on each other in the forest.

"Everything okay, Megan?"

She snapped out of her reverie with a jolt. Sean Bertram lowered himself to sit on his heels beside her, those startling blue eyes smiling. "I just want to check with you on what we'll be doing once we get to this cabin. I understand you're going to dress up and play hostess?"

"Oh ... yes." Megan patted her knapsack. "I've got my dress right here. There won't be room in the cabin for very many at a time. So I'll talk to everybody outside first, then I understand you're to bring the kids inside, in small groups. When I finish, Peter will show them around outside."

"All right," he said. "That sounds easy enough to manage." He stood up. "You have any idea what happened to Jeremy James? He sure left in a hurry."

Megan murmured something noncommittal, thinking of Soo Yun and the way Jeremy James had messed up her stay at camp, maybe even her life. Sean got up and wandered off to talk to somebody else. She watched him go, wishing she'd been able to switch the subject in some clever way ... anything to keep him talking to her. Willow would have. She sighed. Still, he was nearby. And the hike was a long way from over.

"Okay. Time to go," called Miss Loring.

Megan got to her feet. She and Peter threaded their way among campers resting on the ground or on fallen logs and started on. One by one the hikers joined the line zigzagging up the ridge. The way leveled out at the top where the other side of the ridge dropped away into another valley.

After a while the trail looped into an open, rocky area where few trees grew. Across the valley, sheer cliffs lifted to glacier-splotched peaks slicing into the blue sky. Streams tumbled in filmy skeins from the glaciers to the forest thousands of feet below.

The sound of rushing water filled the air. In the valley bottom a stream bubbled around rocks in foam-streaked swirls. From this place the mountains looked as they must always have looked ... except for a spot on the valley floor almost hidden from their sight by a bulge of rock. Megan frowned, keeping her eye on that spot as they moved across the open area.

Then the trail swung out and she could see down, past the bulge of rock. She stopped so suddenly Peter ran into her. "Oh no!" she exclaimed. "Look!"

Peter looked. "That's the same road we saw. And that must be the truck we heard."

Miss Loring passed a knot of hikers and came to stand beside Megan and Peter. She followed their gaze. Then, her voice incredulous, she said, "There are laws to protect the stream banks. How can they get away with that?"

Far below, a yellow bulldozer roared to life. It had

already scraped shrubs and debris from the forest floor into great ugly heaps. Now its noise drowned out the rushing of the water. Where a raw gouge scarred the stream bank, mud stained the clear water and drifted downstream. Trees lay toppled in a clearing. Some lay partly in the stream.

As she gazed at the destruction, Megan felt like crying. She wanted to fly down the mountain to where the men were working and scream at them to stop. But they probably owned the land and had a perfect right to do what they were doing.

She was only one person. What could she do?

Threaked opening to watch what was going on
in the valley. Though at first Miss Loring had
appeared shocked and angry, she quickly com-
posed her expression and kept her voice neutral.

"Understand," she said to the students, "we don't
know what those people plan to do here. They'd have to
have permits to clear the land. However, from what
you've learned about water quality and taking care of
the ecosystem, is there anything you'd point out to
them if you could?"

"They're cutting down the trees where the birds and
squirrels live," said a skinny boy who'd hopped up on a
rock for a better look.

Another boy with thick glasses scowled and gestured toward the machine. "Bulldozing the forest floor
like that means they're destroying plants that are home
and food and protection for lots of living things."

"Well, I think," Tikela announced, "that someone
ought to tell them that the dirt that's washing into the
stream will kill the insects. Then the fish can't live
there."

"And if they cut down the trees along the creek,"
added someone from Peter's cabin, "there'll be nothing
to hold the soil in place, and the banks will erode."

The discussion made Megan feel a little better. She wasn't the only one upset by what was happening below. But the workers were a long way down a very steep mountainside, and there was no trail. Right now she couldn't make her opinion known to those men, even if they would listen.

During the discussion, Peter had been snapping pictures of the project below them. Now he turned to her. "Megan, do you think I should go on ahead and tell that old miner, Jack McCracken, that we're on our way?"

"Good idea," Megan said, glad for something else to think about. "I'll go with you. I need time to get into my costume before the kids get there."

Peter got a go-ahead from one of the teachers. He and Megan slipped away, leaving the group still watching the loggers. The noise of the bulldozer faded. They hiked in silence for a while.

"I can't wait to meet Jack McCracken," Megan said. "Jodi Marsh told me that he's spent his whole life prospecting. He was really disappointed when modern costs and government regulations kept him from getting his ore to market. I wonder what *he* thinks about those men messing up the woods so close to Morning Gulch?"

Peter shrugged. They followed a long ridge, then switchbacked down a steep hillside to a clear, shallow stream—probably the same one that bubbled through the valley where the loggers were working, Megan thought. Peter went ahead along the creek until they came to a path which led up a brushy slope and past some big hemlocks.

The trail entered a clearing where an old log cabin perched near the edge of a gully. "Oh, what a lovely, peaceful place!" Megan breathed deeply, gazing up at the surrounding peaks.

Peter walked closer to the cabin. "Jack! Jack McCracken, are you here?" he called.

"Tarnation! Who's making all that noise?" A wiry little man in a plaid flannel shirt and battered felt hat appeared at the edge of the woods across the clearing. "Just widening the trail to the old stable," he said. His rusty beard split in a wide grin that told them he wasn't nearly as crotchety as he sounded. "You kids from the school camp?"

Megan nodded. "I'm Megan Parnell, and this is my stepbrother, Peter Lewis. Your friend Jodi told us how this place looked when you first found it. She said you'd put a new roof and chimney on the cabin, and cut the brush down. You've really been busy, Mr. McCracken."

"Call me Jack, young lady." He looked around the clearing with pride. "I'm glad to have something to do. Had to shut my mining down, you know."

"Jodi told us about that too."

"We saw that somebody's built a road and is clearing land not far from here," Peter said.

"Yup. Durn developers."

"Do you know their plans?"

"Going to build a resort there, they told me."

"A resort!" wailed Megan. "Out here in the wilderness?"

Jack shrugged. "Guy said they'll have cabins and a big dining room. Place for flatlanders to come and 'experience' the mountains, that's what he said."

"That might not be so bad," ventured Peter. "They'd probably like to visit the Gulch."

"Yes," Megan said sarcastically. "In all-terrain vehicles. They'll wreck the trail and leave their garbage ..." She stopped. "Sorry. I don't know any such thing. I'm just mad because those men are making such a mess."

"Don't blame you," Jack said. "Why don't you go on in and see how we've fixed up the cabin?"

Megan pushed open the door. "The door works! Jodi told me how they could hardly open it when they first found the cabin, but it doesn't stick now."

"Durn right it doesn't stick." The old man gestured toward the cast iron cookstove in the corner. "The fellows from the historical society fixed the stove and the holes in the floor." He noticed Megan examining the homemade bedstead. "The quilt on that bed was hand-stitched by Lucy Steincroft's mother. I take it off and use my own bedroll at night."

"It's beautiful," she murmured. She fingered the 1910 calendar hanging on the wall, then turned to the table where a candlestick stood beside an old leather Bible. "Jodi said there'd be a Bible exactly like the one Lucy gave her!" she exclaimed. "Everything's so interesting. But I'd better hurry and get dressed. The kids will be here any minute."

"Lucy's room was upstairs," Jack said. "You can change up there."

She ran up some narrow steps to a dark landing. "Ouch!" she exclaimed as she bumped her head on a low rafter. "I forgot Lucy was only a little girl!" She pushed open the shutters on the window beside the landing. Light flooded in.

A child's old-fashioned cloak and bonnet hung from pegs beside the window. Lucy's small bedstead stood under the slanting rafters with a featherbed and quilt on the bed and a rag rug on the floor beside it. On a little homemade table a McGuffey's reader, a candlestick, an ink well, and a wooden penholder with old-fashioned nib seemed to wait for that long-ago child to come back to her lessons.

Megan picked up a photocopy of the letter Lucy had hidden in the rafters and forgotten. It was laminated on both sides with sturdy plastic so visitors could read it for themselves. Megan imagined Jodi's excitement when she'd discovered Lucy's treasure bag with the little wooden doll and the bottle of gold nuggets Lucy's dad had given her. This letter, too, had been in the treasure bag. Megan skimmed the childish scrawl. She blinked back tears when she read the sad postscript about the accident which had killed Lucy's father and made it necessary for her and her mother to leave Morning Gulch.

Megan buttoned herself into the calico dress, hoping she could make Lucy's life seem as real to the campers as it did to her.

"Everybody's here," Peter called from outside.

Megan stuffed her hiking clothes into her knapsack and tied on her sunbonnet, then peeked out the window. The counselors were settling the campers on the ground in front of the cabin. Dozens of them, plus the teachers and the other counselors. And Sean! Suddenly

Megan had more than just butterflies fluttering in her stomach. It felt like a whole flock of sparrows. But she lifted her ankle-length skirts and made her way down the stairs. Taking a deep breath, she opened the door and stepped through.

"Look at Megan!" voices exclaimed. She waited while the buzz of talking died down.

"Welcome to Morning Gulch," she said. She gulped another big breath. "I'd like to invite you to step back in time to the year 1910. For more than thirty years, prospectors in these mountains have been seeking the fabulous gold they hope will make them rich. One of them, Julius Steincroft, found gold in Morning Gulch up there." Megan pointed through the trees toward the mountain that towered over the valley. "He built this cabin and brought his wife and daughter to live here.

"But he never got a chance to become rich. Shortly after his family arrived, Julius was killed in a mine cave-in. His little girl, Lucy, and her mother went to live in the town of Bayside."

Megan told how the home had stood abandoned until Jodi Marsh, her brother, and cousin took shelter in it from a storm and how Jodi's discovery of the treasure bag helped them find Lucy—by that time an elderly woman in the Bayside nursing home. The campers listened intently.

"Lucy became Jodi's very good friend. It thrilled her that people like us would visit her old home in the mountains. Before she died, she gave some of her keepsakes to Jodi to show what pioneer life was like. You'll see them in the cabin."

Miss Loring came to stand beside Megan and beckoned to Jack McCracken to stand. "This is Mr. Jack McCracken," the young teacher said. "He's a real miner and he takes care of the cabin. It's his home, and you are his guests, so look but don't touch. Sean will take you inside, a group at a time. Then Peter will show you the stable where Lucy helped her father hide his ore samples. While you wait for your turn, you can eat your lunch and talk to Mr. McCracken. Then we'll all hike to the mine."

As Sean led the first group past Megan into the cabin, he spoke just loud enough for her to hear. "Nice speech, Megan. You look cute in that dress!"

Megan blushed, but managed a smile. "Thank you." Her heart sang his compliment over and over as the campers entered and looked around. She told each group about the furnishings, then led the way upstairs and retold the story of Lucy's treasure bag.

Once she glanced out the window to see Peter bringing a group back along Jack's trail from the ruins of the stable. Other campers clustered around Jack McCracken, hanging on to every word of his tales. Megan could tell the old miner was having the time of his life.

Hanna Joy came in with the last group. Her face seemed pale, and she'd lost some of her bounce. "Are you all right?" Megan asked as they climbed the stairs.

"A little tired, that's all." Hanna Joy gestured around Lucy's room. "I wish Soo Yun could see this."

"Me too," Megan answered. She wondered if Soo Yun

would still be at camp when they returned.

When the last of the group left the cabin, Megan changed back into her jeans and sweatshirt, closed the shutters, and joined Peter and Sean outside. The counselors and campers had followed Jack McCracken back to the stream and along the trail which led to the Morning Mine.

"Miss Loring said for us to eat our lunch, then come along," Peter told her, taking another bite out of his tuna sandwich.

"All right. I'm starved," Megan answered. She bowed her head briefly to thank God for the food and for helping her with her talk.

When she raised her head, she saw Sean watching. He looked from her to Peter. He must have seen Peter pray too. "Religious nuts, huh?" Sean's voice teased, but his words made Megan blush. Maybe she should pretend she hadn't heard—but she had. She smiled, looking him straight in the eye.

"Since when is a person nuts to be thankful for good things?"

Now it was Sean's turn to blush. "I didn't mean ... It's just that people usually say grace at a table ..."

"Maybe so. But Jesus prayed wherever He happened to be. I guess we can too."

"Okay, I'm sorry. Can we forget it?" Sean turned away and took a drink from his water bottle.

A little amazed—and worried—that she'd come on so strong, Megan changed the subject. "You did a great job of keeping everybody in order, Sean. I was glad you were there."

"No problem."

She turned to her stepbrother. "How did your part of the tour go, Peter?"

"There's really not much to see. I explained how the stable was dug into the side of the hill and told how Jodi and the boys hunted for the nuggets Lucy and her father hid there. They all thought the story about her falling through the roof was really funny."

"Maybe Jack can rebuild the stable someday," Megan said. "Speaking of Jack, we'd better get going or we'll miss seeing what he's done at the mine."

Sean held out a big plastic bag. "Toss your garbage in here with everyone else's. I get to pack it all out again."

Megan tied her water bottle to her belt and pocketed her trail mix. The rest she tossed into Sean's sack.

Peter set a rapid pace along the creek, across the foot log, and up toward Morning Gulch. Plainly, he didn't care much for Sean's company. To cover what seemed to her an awkward silence, Megan asked Sean about the upcoming student elections.

"I was student body president last year," he said. "This year I'll run for sophomore class president. Next year, maybe Madrona High's student body president."

Sean *did* have confidence. "Congratulations," Megan said. "What do you want to do as class president?"

"Haven't given it much thought yet. Probably try to get more voice for our class in school policy, greater choice of subjects ... that sort of thing."

"Oh."

Sean flashed one of his brilliant smiles at her. "You'll vote for me, won't you?"

Megan smiled back, teasingly. "Maybe. First I'll have to see what your opposition has to say."

He went on, ignoring what she'd said. "But if I get into student government again this year, I'd have a good chance at the top office next year, even if I'll only be a junior."

"And," Megan finished for him, "that would look great on a college application."

Sean shot a look at her, as if uncertain whether she was serious or making fun of him. He seemed to decide she was serious and nodded.

Peter was far ahead. They climbed faster while Megan thought over the exchange. Something about Sean's attitude disturbed her. He was probably right about junior high politics but, after all, a person doesn't learn how to make good big decisions without making many good small decisions first. She sighed. Sean was *so* handsome.

Finally they reached the foot of the tailings that had tumbled from the mouth of the Morning Mine. Above them campers filed out of the mine behind Jack McCracken. They called to Megan, Peter, and Sean when they saw them scrambling up past the slope of waste rock. Beyond the campers, Megan could see where Jack had braced the mine entrance with new timbers.

Tikela ran to Megan. "We followed the tunnel all the way to the airshaft. Jack told us how he lowered Jodi down into it on a rope to hunt for her brother and cousin."

"That must have been scary," Megan answered. "But

Jodi said Jack stayed right there and pulled all of them out of the mine."

Hanna Joy joined them. She leaned her head against Megan's arm. "I'd never be that brave," she said.

"You are brave," Megan told her. "Just in a different way. Besides, Jodi said she didn't feel courageous. She was scared to death, but she said Jesus helped her."

Hanna Joy's face looked paler than before, but she smiled. "I know. He helps me too."

One of the male counselors called for attention. "Mr. McCracken says he'll take anyone who wants to see the airshaft from the top. If you are tired, you can wait here."

Most of the campers decided they'd go with Jack, but some of them decided to wait. As Megan scrambled up the rocky mountainside past the mine entrance, she looked back to see Hanna Joy and several other girls exploring near the mine. Nearby, one of the counselors sat talking to a group of resting students.

Megan walked up to a newly built railing around the airshaft, a square black hole dropping into the interior of the earth. She imagined Jodi's terrifying ride in a rope sling over the edge of the rock and into the blackness of the mine. Jodi hadn't known if she'd find the boys dead or alive. She listened to Jack telling the story to the campers.

Sean leaned on the railing and peered into the shaft. "Lucky that Jodi's brother and cousin weren't killed in the explosion that trapped them."

Well, Megan thought, I've been brave so far. I might as well try again. "Jodi says it was God, not luck," she answered. "She said she learned something very important that day."

"What was that?"

"God goes with His children everywhere."

Sean looked at her as if about to crack a joke. Instead, he turned and called to the kids, "Okay, everybody. We've got a long hike home ahead of us. Let's get going."

As the campers started back, Megan walked over to Jack McCracken. "Thank you, Jack. We'll never forget today."

Jack's eyes twinkled. "When I first saw your friend Jodi and her sidekicks looking like three drowned rats, I never thought this old hermit prospector would be telling stories to kids like them ... or that I'd enjoy it. Thanks yourself, and say 'hi' to Jodi when you get back."

As she slid down the rocks past the mine entrance, Megan saw Peter at the top of the tailings pile, snapping pictures of the hikers moving down Morning Gulch toward the creek. Megan waved to Jack as he started after the kids, then walked over to Peter.

"Great hike, Megan!" Peter lowered his camera and gave her a high five.

"Isn't this beautiful?" Megan swung around, taking in the panorama of the mine behind her with Morning Gulch running on up to a narrow pass in the peaks. The forested valley below spread out between them and the mountains beyond. "Oh, Peter, a big resort so close to Morning Gulch would spoil the whole feeling of this place! How can we stop those men?"

"We? You mean you and me? Who'd listen to us?"

"Probably no one," Megan agreed. "But if all those kids down there got involved too, maybe we could do something." She watched the colorful line of hikers weaving in and out among the boulders. The leaders had almost reached the woods.

Peter snapped his camera into its case. "We'd better go."

"Okay. I want to keep an eye on Hanna Joy. She seemed awfully tired." Megan frowned. "Wait a minute, Peter. I don't see her pink bandanna, do you?"

He searched the line. "No. Did she go back to the cabin?"

"I don't think so. She was with some other girls when we went to the shaft."

Peter ran back to the mine entrance and called her name. "I don't think she'd have gone in there alone," he said. "Maybe somebody took her on ahead."

They started along the trail. Megan looked back, searching the rocky outcrops and tumbled boulders, but saw nothing. "Peter, why don't you go on and check with the teachers? I'll wait, in case she's still up here someplace."

Peter's blue eyes mirrored her concern. "All right. Watch for me. If she's there, I'll wave from the edge of the woods."

Then he was gone, leaving Megan alone on the mountainside.

The air felt autumn brisk. Nighttime temperatures could drop below freezing this time of year. "Lord, let her be okay," Megan prayed. She glanced up to check the position of the sun and, despite her worry, caught her breath at what she saw.

High cirrus clouds swirled in a gauzy veil across the sky, making a gossamer whirlpool which caught the sun's rays in a misty wheel of rainbow circling the sun. The sun's rays, striking through ordinary raindrops, caused ordinary rainbows, she remembered. Cirrus clouds were made of tiny ice particles. Maybe the bits of ice in the clouds acted the same as raindrops.

Whatever, she knew these high, feathery clouds often brought a weather change. Remembering the sudden storm that had caught Jodi and the boys two summers ago, Megan hoped that the change would wait until everyone was safely back at Camp Galena.

"Lord, I hope Hanna Joy is waiting at the cabin, but just in case she isn't, where would she have gone?" Megan scanned the wall of the gulch above. No flash of pink up there, but maybe if she climbed one of those outcroppings of rock, she'd see more.

She scurried up the sun-warmed rock on hands and feet. Far below, Peter trotted to catch up with the campers now disappearing into the woods. Panting from her scramble, Megan sat down to wait for his signal. She let her eyes roam over the nooks and crannies of the gulch's wall. Nothing.

She waited for what seemed an age. Where was Peter? Finally, she saw him come out of the woods and stand looking up toward the mine. She hopped up and waved both arms.

He spread his arms wide in a *Nothing!* gesture, then turned and went back into the trees.

"She's not there!" Megan whispered to herself. "Oh, Hanna Joy, where are you?"

H anna Joy!" Megan shouted the missing girl's name with all her strength. Then, choking back a sob, she clawed herself higher up the steep granite side of the gulch. Again her eyes combed the tumbled boulders below and to either side. Nothing.

Suddenly she jerked her head back to the left. There in that little hollow! Behind a rock, a bit of pink glimmered.

"Hanna Joy! Hanna Joy!" Megan slipped and slid down the granite slope and clambered over rocks to the hidden hollow. Hanna Joy turned her head as Megan neared. She stretched out her arms, tears running down her cheeks.

"Megan, I was praying someone would come!"

Megan dropped to her knees and hugged the younger girl. "Are you hurt?"

"Not hurt," Hanna Joy told her. "We were exploring. I didn't feel good, so I told the others to go on. I fell asleep. When I woke up, everyone was gone. Oh, Megan, I was so scared!"

"Do you feel better now?"

With effort, Hanna Joy got to her feet. "I don't know. I'm awful tired ... like the last time I had to go to the hospital." She took a few unsteady steps and sagged against Megan.

"Oh, Hanna Joy!" Megan felt like crying. "We'll get you

out of here. Peter's gone for help."

"I'm embarrassed to make someone come back for me."

"Don't worry about that," Megan told her. The two girls sat down in the shelter of a big rock. A cool breeze stirred the grasses. Hanna Joy began to shiver, so Megan helped her put on the jacket she wore tied around her waist. Then they leaned back to wait for someone to come. The rocks would hold the sun's heat for a while, Megan thought. But evening was only a few hours off. Would they be able to get Hanna Joy back to camp?

"You know the worst part of being sick?" Hanna Joy stared into the sky, speaking almost to herself. "It's having no hair. I can make it through the pain and the throwing up. But kids at school say things. They think I don't hear them, but I do."

Megan watched the filmy clouds beginning to veil the sun, remembering Hanna's "happy face" surprise for Tikela. "You handle it so well. No one would know it bothers you."

"If I pretend it's no big deal, it's easier for other kids and it's easier for me. But I don't like to be different."

"No one likes being different."

"You know the best part of being sick?"

Megan swallowed hard. "What?"

"It's learning what's really important and what's not. Like us being friends. And like listening to God. You know what He tells me through that rainbow in the clouds up there?"

"To have hope?"

"Well, yes. But that's a special rainbow. I've never seen one like it."

92

"I think it's called a corona." Megan traced with her eyes the bands of color shimmering around the sun, being careful not to look directly at the brilliant disk itself. "It's a circle. Is that what you mean?"

"Yes. Why is a circle important?"

Megan felt like she was a student, Hanna Joy the teacher. "I suppose ... because it's a perfect shape. It has no beginning, no end."

"Right. Like God. Like life."

"Like life?"

"Yes. My mom told me once that a Christian's life is like a circle. God knows about us before we're born, and life doesn't end when we die. We keep on living in heaven."

"Oh Hanna Joy, you're right! That's why Jesus came, to give us eternal life."

"Yes. I hope I get to grow up, Megan. But I'm not afraid to die."

Megan blinked away tears. She hopped up on some boulders to see if anyone was coming. No one. "God, make them hurry," she whispered.

Hanna Joy stood up too. "Megan, I feel better now. If you help me get back to the trail I think I can make it."

Megan didn't object. If Hanna Joy could keep moving, she'd stay warmer.

When they'd reached the trail Hanna Joy dropped to the ground and sat trembling. "Just let me rest a minute," she panted. Soon she got up again. Leaning on Megan's arm, she moved slowly along the trail.

Far down the gulch, shouts echoed. Megan saw two figures coming toward them—one, Mr. Edgebert, the other, Sean. She waved. Hanna Joy tried to wave too, but her knees buckled. Megan steadied her and helped her sit down on a boulder.

The two figures paused, but when they saw the girls waiting, they hurried on. Sean jogged up to the girls well ahead of middle-aged Mr. Edgebert.

"Whew, that was a workout!" he said, wiping the sweat from his forehead with his sleeve. "You really scared us," he said to Hanna Joy. "Where'd you find her, Megan?"

"Up there." Megan nodded toward the wall above them. "She's very tired. I don't think she can make it back to camp."

"That's a problem, isn't it?" Sean dropped his pack on the trail. "We brought the first aid kit, in case she was hurt."

Mr. Edgebert arrived. Taking in the situation at a glance, he bent to feel Hanna Joy's pulse.

He straightened and spoke quietly to Sean, who nodded. "Madam, your chariot awaits," Mr. Edgebert said to Hanna Joy as Sean knelt in front of her. "All aboard."

Sean stood up again, Hanna Joy clinging piggyback to his broad shoulders. Megan watched Sean start off. Hanna Joy wasn't tall, but she was chunky. How far could he carry her before tiring? Megan picked up the knapsack Sean had dropped and turned to Mr. Edgebert.

"Hanna Joy's leukemia has been in remission," she told him. "Do you think she's had a relapse?"

The teacher looked worried, but he spoke casually. "She probably just pushed herself too hard. Thanks, Megan, for noticing she was missing. Miss Loring said

94

she'd assumed Hanna Joy was with you. No one would have known differently until we counted noses."

Megan and Mr. Edgebert followed while Sean picked his slow way down the trail. Hanna Joy's head drooped against his shoulder.

Sean turned and Megan glimpsed the girl's white face. "How's she doing?" Sean asked. "I can't get her to say much."

"This is hard on her. We could make a stretcher and carry her out," Mr. Edgebert said, as if thinking out loud. "But that's slow. We need to get her to her doctor, soon."

"Does Jack McCracken have a citizen's band radio?" asked Sean.

"I didn't see one," said Megan. "If he did we could call the Search and Rescue people. They could send a helicopter."

"Megan, would you run on ahead and tell Miss Loring and the other staff members what's happened? Tell them to send somebody for help, then start the other kids down the trail."

"All right." Megan squeezed Hanna Joy's shoulder. "You'll soon be at Lucy's cabin," she told her. "Hang on."

" 'Bye, Megan. I love you."

"Love you too, Hanna Joy."

Megan blinked the mist out of her eyes and sprinted down the gulch. Peter met her at the log crossing. "You found her?"

Megan nodded. The other campers waited near the cabin. Miss Loring saw her and beckoned to Jack McCracken and the other two teachers. Megan relayed

Mr. Edgebert's message. Jack confirmed that he had no radio or telephone.

"I could run ahead to the road," Peter offered. "I could flag somebody down ... ask them to send word to Search and Rescue."

"He shouldn't go alone," Megan said. "Let me go too."

Miss Loring hesitated, looking at the other teachers.

"If anything happened to them, we'd be responsible for letting them go off alone," one teacher said.

"True, but we need the adults to supervise the campers," said Miss Loring.

"I can't keep up with these two for long," Jack McCracken told Miss Loring. "But I can come along behind to help if something should happen. How would that be?"

"Well ... okay," she answered. "All right, Megan, Peter, you're off."

They grabbed their knapsacks from the cabin. Jack McCracken picked up his walking stick, and they headed for the trail. The young people soon outdistanced Jack, racing each other up the switchbacks to the top of the ridge. Megan stopped and leaned against a tree, her heart pounding.

"We'd better slow down," Peter gasped. "Won't do Hanna Joy any good if we collapse."

Megan drew a great breath of air into her burning lungs. "You're right. But it's a long way to the road. By the time we get word out, it will be almost dark."

They jogged along the ridge top. "Listen," Megan said. She slowed and Peter slowed too. "The bulldozer is still working."

The same idea hit them both at once. The road! Those men had a truck—and maybe a two-way radio.

They started to run and soon burst into the open area where they'd watched the developers working earlier in the day. The bulldozer roared on, still pushing debris into huge piles. More old-growth trees had been felled. Men were lopping off the branches with their chain saws. With more of the trees down, Megan saw a small building she hadn't noticed earlier, a boxy white trailer office like those used at construction sites.

"Hey! Hey!" Megan and Peter jumped up and down, yelling, but the men were making too much noise to hear them.

"I think we could get down over there." Megan pointed to the edge of the steep, rocky slope where shrubs grew thick enough to offer handholds.

"How will we get through that brush along the creek?"

"There's not much brush if we climb down there to the left, then wade across."

"We'd better tell Jack," Peter said.

"Tell me what?"

"Oh, Jack, hi! We thought we were way ahead of you!"

Jack chuckled. "Remember the story about the tortoise and the hare?"

"We had an idea," Megan explained. "We thought those loggers might have a radio or cell phone to call for help."

The old miner pushed his battered hat back so his pale forehead showed. He studied the slope below.

"Would sure save time. But it's tricky footing. Be careful. And if you reach those men, let them know that

I'm watching from up here."

Megan and Peter picked their way down the steep mountainside, grasping rocks and bushes to keep their balance. Then they were slipping and sliding through trees. They came to a gash in the rocks through which a small stream tumbled on its way to the creek. The sheer sides were wet with spray.

They followed the edge of the ravine until they came to a fallen tree lying diagonally across the cleft. Beyond the tree, a steep ridge of rock blocked progress on their side of the ravine. Megan pulled herself up on the massive trunk of the windfall and studied the lay of the land.

"If we cross the ravine on this tree," she told Peter, "I think we can reach the creek by following the other side."

"I guess we'll have to try," he said. "We can't go any farther on this side."

Megan stepped out onto the log and inched her way across, trying not to look into the narrow, dark chasm. The log shifted a little under her weight and her heart jumped into her throat. Behind her, Peter sat down to straddle the log. He scooted his way across. Once he knocked a piece of bark loose. It splashed into the stream just as Megan hopped safely onto solid rock.

When they reached the creek at the bottom of the hill, they removed their boots and stepped into the icy water.

"Brrr! Any colder, it would be frozen," said Peter. They splashed across to a strip of sandy beach. Megan looked up toward the trail to see if Jack was watching. He waved his walking stick.

The noise of the bulldozer ceased abruptly. "Uh-oh. Bet it's quitting time," Peter said.

Megan glanced at the sun, which had dropped close to the mountain peaks. "Hurry! Put on your boots." She finished lacing hers and started to run.

She raced around the bend. A man in a hard hat squatted near a fallen tree which lay with its top in the streambed, adjusting something on his chain saw. He straightened and started up the muddy bank, chain saw in hand.

"Wait," she shouted. "Please wait."

The man whirled, almost losing his balance. "Well, I'll be! Where'd you come from?"

"Up there," she panted, pointing. Peter thudded up behind her. "We're with a group of school campers. One of the children got sick at Morning Gulch and can't hike out. Can you help us?"

"Hey Jeb, Stan. Come here." The two loggers worked their way toward them over logs and branches. They stared. "These kids climbed down that hillside." The first logger gestured toward Jack. "That a friend of yours up there?"

They nodded. The first man told Jeb and Stan about the sick camper, then turned back to Megan and Peter. "How do you expect us to help?"

"We hoped you might have a phone or radio to call the Search and Rescue people," Megan said.

"No, sorry."

"Well, there's a radio phone at Camp Galena. You could get there much faster in your truck than we could on the trail, and the people at camp could call them."

"I guess we can do that. Good thing you caught us."

Jeb, the oldest of the three men, spoke. "We're quitting early today. Another five minutes, we'd have been gone. Where's the sick kid?"

Megan and Peter gave them the details and thanked them, then retraced their steps to where they'd crossed the creek. As they labored back up the mountainside, Megan prayed that the message would get through. The men had been polite enough, though not overly eager to help.

She had plenty of time to think about the damage the men were doing to the forest. If only Hanna Joy hadn't needed their help! She'd have told them what she thought of their project.

When Megan and Peter finally reached the trail, the last of the campers were straggling by. Megan looked for Sean but didn't see him. Mr. Edgebert was talking to Jack McCracken.

"I'm glad I didn't know what you two were up to," Mr. Edgebert said, turning to Megan and Peter. "But thanks. We saw the truck leave. I assume the men agreed to take the message?"

Megan nodded. "How is Hanna Joy?"

"She's resting in the cabin. Miss Loring is with her," Mr. Edgebert said. "Megan, Miss Loring says she's sure you and Willow can manage your campers without her if she doesn't get back tonight."

"Oh. Yes, I think we can."

They made their farewells to the old prospector. "If you ever get to Madrona Bay, come and see us," Megan told him.

"Thanks, young lady. Whatever happens, I've a feeling I'll be seeing more of you." Jack jerked his head toward the scarred valley floor. "You kids will probably be trying to do something about that next!"

Somebody should do something, Megan thought as they left Jack standing on the trail. But what could be done?

Battle Strategy

The hike back to the road was mostly downhill. Even so, Megan felt weary all over. Her calf muscles, especially, ached as she, Peter, and Mr. Edgebert hiked from the darkening woods to the campers waiting for them on the bus.

Suddenly the thumping clatter of a helicopter made her forget her weariness. As the craft flew overhead, she read the words "Search and Rescue" on its side. It turned away from the road and flew over the ridges toward Morning Gulch.

"Good," said Peter. "The loggers did take our message to camp. Hanna Joy will have help soon."

On the bus, Sean motioned to Megan, patting the empty seat beside him. "Sit here."

Her heart jumped as Sean's blue eyes smiled into hers. She sat down, letting her knapsack slip to the floor.

"I saw you talking to the loggers by the creek. That must have been a pretty tough hike."

Megan looked down at her dirty jeans and the scratches on her arms. "It was. But carrying Hanna Joy all that way couldn't have been easy, either."

Sean leaned back with his hands behind his head and stretched his back and shoulders. "Yeah. I'll feel it tomorrow. This camp counseling's turned out to be harder than I expected."

"It's fun, though, isn't it?"

"I guess." He changed the subject abruptly. "Megan, have you ever thought of running for school office?"

"No. Why?"

"I've been watching you. You're good at getting things done. I think we'd work well together. How would you like to run as my vice president?"

She looked at him, speechless. He lounged against the window, one tanned arm flung over the back of the seat, studying her seriously.

"I'm not one of the popular kids, Sean."

"A little public relations would take care of that. We'll plaster posters around school with your name and face."

Sean continued to describe his plans. Megan's mind whirled with delight and confusion. He wanted to work with ... be with ... her! Then other thoughts intruded. Sean's put down of Peter. His whole reason for wanting to be in school politics. She'd better move slowly.

"Thanks for asking." She smiled. "I'll think about it."

A short while later the bus pulled into Camp Galena's parking lot. Mr. Davis, the director, greeted the hikers as they climbed off the bus. "Megan, I'm told you and Peter played a big part in getting word to us about Hanna Joy. Can you two come to the staff building? I need to find out just what happened."

"But my campers ..." Megan began.

"I've already asked Mrs. Sturgelewski, the camp nurse, to stand in for you and Miss Loring."

"Oh, thank you. How's Soo Yun?"

"She seems to be fine. She spent most of the afternoon with the other tour group."

The rest room was full of girls cleaning up after the hike. Megan quickly washed her face and hands, then hurried to Tamarack to put on clean jeans and a sweatshirt. She heard Willow's voice upstairs.

"Hello," she called from the porch. Willow stuck her head over the half-wall. "Mrs. Sturgelewski's going to be here with my girls for a while," Megan told her. "I'll see you at dinner."

Mr. Edgebert and Peter were already in Mr. Davis' office when she got there. They told what had happened.

"The school district may want you to make official statements later," said Mr. Davis. "But it sounds like no carelessness was involved. Megan, Peter, you acted creatively to avert what could have been a serious problem.

"I've notified Hanna Joy's parents. They'll be waiting for her at the hospital. I expect Miss Loring will bring word on her condition when she returns."

"I hope Hanna Joy's leukemia hasn't come back," said Megan.

"We all hope that," Mr. Davis answered. "Have we covered everything you think might be important?"

"All but one thing ..." Megan said.

"Yes!" said Peter. "Tell him about those developers."

So they explained to the camp director about the resort to be built near Morning Gulch and the careless practices of the developers. "I feel funny complaining," Megan said, "when they were good enough to get the message about Hanna Joy to you."

Mr. Davis looked thoughtful. "We're working hard here at Camp Galena to educate people about taking care of our resources. It sounds as if they may be ignoring environmental regulations. I'll ask somebody to look into it."

At dinner Megan ate extra helpings of everything, though Soo Yun, she noticed, ate very little. Mr. Davis announced there'd be a half-hour of free time before the evening campfire began. The dining hall quickly emptied of everyone but the girls of Tamarack cabin, who'd drawn KP duty for that meal.

"Soo Yun's lucky!" Tikela said, wiping a tabletop. "She doesn't have to do KP."

"She won that contest yesterday, fair and square," Laurel answered. "Besides, with all of us working together this won't take long."

"Megan, you run along and talk to Soo Yun," said Mrs. Sturgelewski. "Willow and I can supervise here."

"Thanks," she said, grateful for the nurse's insight. Megan knew that on top of everything else, Soo Yun was worried about Hanna Joy.

As Megan turned to go, she met Willow's eyes and felt an unpleasant shock. Her gaze was smokey with resentment. Was Willow angry because Megan didn't have to supervise KP? Or had she found out that she'd sat with Sean on the bus? Megan shrugged. She had more pressing things to think about right now.

She caught up to Soo Yun. "Want to go for a walk?"

A half smile brightened the younger girl's solemn face. "That would be nice. Megan, what's happening to Hanna Joy?"

"Well, by now she's probably trying to explain to her doctor why she went on such a long hike and got so tired."

"Do you think she'll get well?"

Megan's own heart felt heavy with worry, but she looked for a way to reassure Soo Yun. "I'm praying she will," Megan answered. "You know Hanna Joy. She bounces back like a little rubber ball."

Soo Yun giggled. Suddenly she seemed her old self again. They walked along in companionable silence.

"What about you, Soo Yun? Do you feel better now?"

Soo Yun nodded. "Mrs. Sturgelewski talked with me for a long time. Then my parents came, and we all talked together." She looked up. "My parents are filing charges against Jeremy James. He might have to go to jail. But I'm glad I told. Maybe because I told, he won't bother other kids."

"I think you did the right thing," Megan said.

The girls had circled through the camp while they walked. As they neared the amphitheater, a bell rang to call everyone to the campfire. Miss Chang, a tiny, energetic woman who taught biology at Madrona High, had arrived and was setting up her slide projector. Mr. Davis finished hanging the "screen," the white sheet used for last night's skit, as campers came pouring into the amphitheater.

Megan's heart leaped as Sean seated himself with some of his boys in the row just ahead. He threw her a wave, then scooted over to make room for another counselor and more campers. The counselor was Willow, and though she sat down directly in front of Megan, she had eyes only for Sean.

They sang a few camp songs while the last of the daylight faded. The camp director introduced Miss

Chang, then turned the lanterns low.

The visitor stood to one side of the makeshift screen with a remote control switch in her hand and began her slide show with a picture of majestic old-growth evergreens. "Imagine for a moment that you are one of the first explorers to see the Pacific Northwest," she said. "Everywhere you look, you see towering evergreen trees. That great forest covers an area of seventy thousand square miles, from the tip of the Alaskan panhandle all the way to the big redwoods of California."

Willow sighed and rolled her eyes at Sean. She crossed her knees and folded her arms in an elaborate show of boredom. A couple of her campers glanced at her, then copied her pose.

"The trees here at camp are second growth," Miss Chang continued. "They are not part of that original forest, although you can find the stumps of some trees that once were." She flashed a picture of a burned-out hulk of a stump, its base encircled by a group of last year's campers, arms outstretched and fingers touching. Megan recognized the stump as one that stood near Tamarack cabin.

"Though most of the great forests are gone," Miss Chang said, "many people still make their living in the timber industry. So we have a big argument. Some people want to continue cutting the old growth. Others wish to save what's left of the big trees as a heritage for future generations and for the sake of the wild creatures who live there."

Willow carried on a whispered conversation with Sean while Miss Chang showed pictures of some of those creatures: deer, black bear, porcupines, and smaller mammals like red squirrels, flying squirrels, shrews, and chipmunks.

Miss Chang paused to glance at Willow, who stopped whispering and sat up straight. Then she clicked the remote, and a picture appeared of a stubby-tailed bird bobbing on the waves of the sea.

"This marbled murrelet is about the size of a robin," she said. "Early in the morning, or at dusk, it leaves the water and wings inland to exchange places with its mate on its nest. No one had ever found one of the nests in Washington until recently, when one was discovered not far from here."

Murmurs came from some of the campers who'd been on the Morning Gulch hike.

"I can tell some of you know about the murrelets," Miss Chang said. She flashed a picture of a downy gray chick huddling in a mossy depression on a tree branch. "The parents of this marbled murrelet chick fly forty or fifty miles inland to where they've hidden their nest high in an old-growth forest."

"Scientists are still learning about the plants and animals that live in the old-growth ecosystem," Miss Chang continued. "They say that as the forests shrink, we're in danger of losing forever many of the creatures that are part of that system."

Megan again thought of the men working near Morning Gulch. At the close of the campfire, Mr. Davis announced that the cooks had hot cocoa and snacks waiting in the mess hall. Megan lingered as the campers hurried out of the amphitheater. No stars showed between the branches tonight. This afternoon's cirrus clouds *had* signaled a change in the weather.

"Coming, Megan?"

"Oh, hi, Peter. I'm coming ... no, wait a minute. Let's tell Miss Chang about those developers."

"Why? What could she do?"

"Probably nothing. I'd just like to talk to her." They climbed over the benches to where Mr. Davis was helping Miss Chang pack her slides. Megan introduced herself. "And this is my stepbrother, Peter Lewis. We really enjoyed your pictures Miss Chang."

"Why, thank you."

"I wish some men we saw today could hear what you had to say," said Megan. "Mr. Davis, did you tell Miss Chang about the project near Morning Gulch?"

"The resort? No. Go ahead and tell her." Mr. Davis picked up her slide projector, and they started toward the mess hall together.

On the way, Megan and Peter told about the tree-cutting and the damage they'd seen to the creek banks. Miss Chang listened, a frown creasing her smooth forehead. "If it's their property," Megan said, "maybe they have the right to do anything they want to with it. But it's close to where the marbled murrelet's nest was found. Besides, they're definitely destroying habitat along the stream bank. I think someone ought to stop them."

Miss Chang put the slides and projector in her car. "I have to go now to be back for my classes tomorrow," she told them. "But if you find out what those men plan and if they are breaking any regulations, come see me.

I'll be interested."

They said good-bye to Miss Chang and went inside the mess hall. Across the room Sean leaned against the wall, smiling down at Willow the same way he'd smiled at Megan that afternoon. Willow darted a glance of triumph her way, but Megan lifted her chin and pretended she didn't see.

Mr. Davis stopped to speak with Mr. Edgebert. He included her and Peter in the conversation. "The Morning Gulch site is a wonderful addition to our outdoor education program," he said. "I'd like to find ways to get the campers more involved."

Seeing Sean and Willow together again had made Megan feel as if someone had just splashed a cup of icy water in her face. But as she listened to Mr. Davis, an idea popped into her head. "I know something they can do ... maybe not this group, but other groups."

"Go on," the camp director encouraged.

"They could make signs to explain about the yew trees, and the marbled murrelet nesting site, and the different plants along the trail."

"Like a nature trail!" Peter exclaimed.

"Good idea!" said Mr. Davis. "Maybe we'll schedule some time tomorrow for the kids to brainstorm more ideas."

Later that night, Megan snuggled deep into her sleeping bag. A few raindrops rattled on the cabin's overhang like tapping fingernails. Mrs. Sturgelewski snored softly in Miss Loring's bed. Most of the girls were so tired from their busy day they'd gone right to sleep.

Pictures flashed across the screen of Megan's brain

like some crazy video. Sean's smile; Willow's jealous glance; Soo Yun's frightened, hurt expression; Hanna Joy's tear-stained face when she found her on the mountain; the bulldozed forest floor; marbled murrelets streaking the long miles to their nesting sites; the cabin at Morning Gulch.

"Lord," she prayed. "Thank You for helping me today. Take care of Hanna Joy. Help me to show Your love to everybody, including Willow ..." Her prayer dissolved into dreaming, and Megan slept.

Somewhere far away a bell rang. Close at hand, thumps and bumps and excited voices burrowed into Megan's consciousness.

"Get up, Megan. Hurry! Time for Clean Cabin inspection."

Megan rolled over and hid her head under her pillow.

Tikela snatched the pillow away. "Come on, lazy bones. My bed's made already."

Megan sat up and shook her groggy head. Mrs. Sturgelewski's sleeping bag was gone, and so was the nurse. Megan groped for her clothes as the chatter continued.

"Last day at camp. It's our last chance to get the award."

"Who's going to check the cabins?"

"Don't know."

"Why did Jeremy James leave, anyway?" asked Laurel. "I liked him."

"I think Soo Yun had something to do with it," one of the other girls replied.

The next words brought Megan wide awake. "What did you do, Soo Yun?"

Soo Yun froze, a sick look on her face.

Megan spoke quickly. "Girls, I know the reason he left. I can't tell you why, but it definitely wasn't Soo Yun's fault."

"Hurry, everybody," Julie interrupted. "I heard people moving around upstairs long before the wake-up bell rang. They got a head start on us."

"That's not fair," wailed Laurel. "Is my bed okay? I've got to find some fresh leaves." She shot out of the cabin. Julie sighed and smoothed her friend's rumpled sleeping bag.

Megan ran through a misty drizzle to the rest room, where she splashed cold water over her face. She frowned at her image in the mirror. The dampness in the air kinked her hair and made it frizzy. She rubbed at her cheek where a fold in the pillow had creased it. "I look awful," she muttered to herself.

Back in the cabin, Julie was frantically sweeping out wet leaves and dirt that had been tracked in. Girls lined spare shoes neatly under the beds and tucked odds and ends into duffle bags.

"Megan, it's almost time for cabin check. Help us!" someone cried.

"I'm sorry, I can't. The campers have to do the work themselves," she said.

"Willow swept the whole floor upstairs," Tikela said. "I heard her tell her kids that Sean will check the cabins."

That figures, Megan thought. And she'll manage to look perfect too, for Sean. "Well, we're going to follow the rules," she told her campers. "You've done a good job. Let's go."

The girls hurried toward the mess hall. Soo Yun lagged behind to wait for Megan. "Thank you for telling them it wasn't my fault Jeremy left," she said. "Megan, what if they ask more questions?"

"You don't have to tell them anything."

"I know. But Mrs. Sturgelewski says that ... that some people do bad things to lots of kids. And most kids think it's their fault, just like I did, so they don't tell anybody. What if Jeremy bothered other kids here?"

Soo Yun was right. She was probably not the first child Jeremy had molested. "Well, if sometime you do decide to talk about it, just remember ... he's the one in the wrong. Not you."

Cheerful voices inside the mess hall and the aromas of bacon, coffee cake, and scrambled eggs made Megan forget the drab morning outside.

"Miss Loring, you're back!" Soo Yun cried, running to the teacher sitting at Tamarack cabin's table. "How is Hanna Joy?"

"Feeling much better. She wanted to return to camp with me this morning."

"Is she still in the hospital?" Megan asked.

"Yes. They're doing some tests this morning but she hopes to go home soon," said Miss Loring. "She said to tell you all she'll see you at school. She wants to know everything you did after she left."

"Did you ride on the helicopter too?" asked a camper.

"Did I ever!" Miss Loring laughed. She took some coffee cake and passed the platter. "The clearing wasn't big enough for the helicopter to land in," she told them. "So the pilot hovered overhead and lowered a paramedic on a rope. We put Hanna Joy in a basket stretcher and they pulled her up. Then the paramedic and I sat on a sort of seat at the end of the rope and held on to each other, spinning and swinging like we were on a carnival ride as they lifted us in. It was scary!"

Tikela played with the food on her plate. "I feel terrible that I teased Hanna Joy our first day here," she told Megan. "I'm going to make a get-well card for our whole cabin to sign."

The door of the mess hall opened and Sean came in. Excitement rippled from table to table as he walked to Mr. Davis and handed him the cabin checklist. From the end of Tamarack's table, Willow flashed Sean a bright smile.

When everyone finished eating, Mr. Davis held up his hand for silence. "We have some important announcements," he said. "First, though, what you've all been waiting for—today's Clean Cabin Award. Sean Bertram, please come and tell us who the best housekeepers at Camp Galena are this morning."

Sean got up, broad-shouldered and smiling, very much at ease. Megan felt all melty inside as she watched him. He held up the polished wood plaque that passed from cabin to cabin. "I thought it would be Cedar Cabin," he said, "until I found pine cones under the counselor's pillow."

"You can't look there!" an indignant squawk rang out.

"Then some people tried to bribe me with candy bars." He patted the bulge in his shirt pocket. Willow's campers giggled. "But plain old hard work and neatness did the trick. Today's winner—first floor, Tamarack Cabin."

Another squawk, this one from Willow. She quickly shut her mouth as Megan's campers erupted in cheers.

While everybody clapped, Sean brought the plaque to their table and gave it to Megan. "I'm honored to present this. Good job, everybody."

The girls craned to see the plaque. Between their heads Megan caught a glimpse of Willow tilting back in her chair, arms folded across her chest. Red spots burned on her cheeks and lightning sparked in her eyes as she glared at Megan.

Mr. Davis called for attention again. "We will go ahead with today's schedule as planned, with a few additions. Mrs. Sturgelewski wants to talk with you for a short while before we are dismissed this morning.

"Also, all of you who went on the Morning Gulch hike yesterday, including the student leaders, will remain here in the mess hall for a short meeting after lunch. Those who went on the field trip will meet in the resource building. We'd like to hear your ideas on how we can make the trips even better.

"The buses will leave for Madrona Bay at 3:00 this afternoon. Now, please give your attention to our very own Mrs. Sturgelewski."

The nurse hopped up on a chair so she could be seen by everybody. "Good morning, campers! I need to talk to you for just a few minutes about a serious subject. I know that most of you learned long ago about 'good' touching and 'bad' touching." Across the table, Soo Yun's face tensed as she looked up at the nurse. Then she lowered her head so her hair hid her face.

Some of the boys snickered. They pretended to slug each other, but Mrs. Sturgelewski ignored them. "A good touch is the kind that shows love and respect and friendship. We all need that kind of touch to feel good about ourselves.

"But there's a touch that does not show love and respect. It's a selfish kind of touching that makes us feel uncomfortable or even bad about ourselves." The boys quit wiggling and fixed their eyes on her. Megan saw kids glancing at each other with expressions on their faces that said, *Why are we talking about this?*

"You have the right to say 'no' to that kind of touching. If some person touches you that way, you have the right to tell someone who can make that person stop.

"I'm sorry to say that here at Camp Galena we had an incident of bad touching," Mrs. Sturgelewski said. "The camper involved did the right thing when she told a teacher."

Soo Yun raised her head a little. Mrs. Sturgelewski talked about people who gain the trust of children. If older people betray their trust by touching them in the wrong way, she explained, kids feel confused. "Maybe the touching even feels good," she said. "But the person betrayed still feels guilty, thinking the abuse is his or her fault. So he keeps silent and tries to forget what happened. But the bad feelings stay there, buried in his memory, and if they aren't dealt with, they can harm him the rest of his life.

"That's why, if anything like this ever happens to you, you should tell someone you trust."

Soo Yun leaned over to Megan. "I'm glad I could trust *you*," she murmured.

"Thank you, Mrs. Sturgelewski," said the camp director. To the campers, Mr. Davis added, "Some of you have already found that our camp nurse is a good person to go to with your problems. But try not to make the sniffles one of them. If this weather continues, be sure to wear your rain gear. Have a good day."

Tikela picked up the plaque from the table. "Can I hang this on our wall?"

"Sure," Megan said. "Congratulations, all of you." Her campers joined the crowd funneling through the exit. Looking sulky, Willow followed them.

"Megan!" Peter called. She walked over to where he stood next to Mr. Davis.

"I wanted to tell you both that I contacted the Department of Natural Resources about the logging you saw yesterday," Mr. Davis said. "Someone's coming by in a short while to check on what they're doing. I'm going with him. I'd like you two to come along."

"Will those people be in trouble?" asked Megan.

"Not necessarily. I just thought you two could be good spokespeople for the concerns of Camp Galena and Morning Gulch."

"Oh." Megan wasn't sure how she felt about confronting the men after they were good enough to help Hanna Joy, but she said, "I'll go."

In the cabin, the girls whose classes were to meet outside were getting into their rain clothes. Megan already had her boots on. She pulled her waterproof jacket and hat out of her duffle bag as Willow came down the stairs behind her campers.

"'Bye!" called Soo Yun as she left with Beth and Tammy. "See you later."

"'Bye. Hurry, Tikela, Julie, Laurel. Oh, Willow,"

called Megan, "Mr. Davis wants me and Peter to go somewhere with him for a little while. Would you tell Miss Loring for me?"

Willow turned, her face scornful. "Aren't you the nice little apple polisher?"

"What?" Megan said. "Willow, what's wrong with you?"

Willow moved into the room and thrust her face close. Her green eyes shot sparks. "You think you can twist everyone around your finger. You got Peter in as student counselor, even though student counselors were supposed to be from the honors classes. You're always trying to tell me and everybody else what to do. And my kids should have won that plaque. What kind of pull... ?"

Megan stiffened. "Stop right there!" she interrupted. "Peter's doing a better job than *some* people I know. And my kids won the award fair and square. I didn't help *my* campers with their work. And I didn't try to bribe Sean with candy bars!"

She caught a glimpse of Julie's and Laurel's scared faces. Tikela looked gleeful.

Willow sucked in her breath. Her eyes narrowed. "Sean likes me! But lately all he can do is talk about you. Why does he think you should be class vice president? You're nobody!"

"Well, maybe I'm nobody, but I'm not a fake."

"A fake?" screeched Willow. "I'll show you who's a fake." She lunged. Megan felt a stinging slap across her face. Then Willow grabbed her hair with both hands and yanked hard.

The shock and pain made Megan gasp. Blindly she reached for Willow. Her hand closed on a fistful of long hair and she yanked too.

"Fight! Fight!" squealed Tikela.

Suddenly Willow let go. A hand gripped Megan's shoulder and shook her. Through tears of anger, she saw Miss Loring gripping Willow with the other hand.

Megan hid her face in her hands and sobbed.

"Sit down, you two." Miss Loring pushed each of them onto a different bunk. "I'm sorry you girls had to see this," she said to Julie, Laurel, and Tikela. "Go on now to your classes."

The campers obeyed, but Tikela paused for a last word. "Megan didn't start it, Miss Loring."

Miss Loring stared at the two. Willow stared back defiantly. Megan gulped and sniffled.

"I really can't believe this," said Miss Loring. "We chose you two as student counselors for your maturity and your example to the younger students. What kind of example is this?"

Shame washed over Megan.

"Willow, I want you to meet my class at the river. Tell them I'll be there shortly. I'll talk to you later."

When Willow had gone, Miss Loring sat down. "Now, what happened?"

"She says I'm kissing-up. And she says I tell everybody else what to do." Megan gulped. "I don't, do I?"

"You're very capable, Megan. Maybe she's mistaking leadership for bossiness. What else?"

Megan felt her face blush. "We both like Sean."

"Oh." Miss Loring smiled a little. "Is he worth a fight?"

"I didn't know there was going to be a fight. What will you do to us, Miss Loring?"

"I think you and Willow need to settle this yourselves."

"She hates me!" Megan wailed.

"Well, you think about it. Meanwhile, comb your hair and go wash your face. I understand Mr. Davis is waiting for you."

Megan ran her brush through her hair, put on her raincoat and hat, and plodded along the trail to the rest room. Her face still stung from Willow's slap. Dismay, embarrassment, and anger churned inside her. "Jesus," she muttered, "I asked You to help me show love to Willow, but all I've done is make her my enemy. How can I show love now?"

Peter waved from beneath the overhanging eaves of the resource building. Megan crossed the open area, dodging puddles, to join him on the porch. Through a window she saw kids at tables working on some kind of nature project. "Mr. Davis is inside," Peter said. "He said to call him when the Department of Natural Resources person comes."

Megan hunched in her vinyl raincoat. She shifted from one foot to the other and peered through the drizzle. "What a gloomy day," she said. "The clouds are almost down to the treetops."

"Yeah. Megan, do you think there's really anything we can do to stop those people from cutting the trees?"

"I don't know," she answered. Her insides still churned over the battle with Willow. She told him what had happened. "Do you think I'm bossy, Peter?"

Peter's grin under his yellow rain hat was teasing. "Aren't most girls bossy?"

"I'm serious. Willow says I tell other people what to do."

"Willow's just jealous."

"Why should she be jealous of me?" Without waiting for an answer, she went on. "Do you think Sean likes me?" Peter didn't respond, so she prodded, "Well? You're in the same cabin with him. Has he said anything?"

Peter looked uncomfortable. "You won't like this,

Megan, but you asked so I'll tell you. I think Sean makes up to you, or Willow, or anybody else who can help him get what he wants."

"He does not!" Megan protested. "How can you say that? Are you sure you're not a teeny bit jealous yourself?"

Peter pressed his lips together and turned away.

"I'm sorry. That was uncalled for," she said. "But you're wrong about Sean." She was positive of that—almost positive, anyway.

"Here's the DNR guy," Peter said as a truck with a Department of Natural Resources emblem on the door wheeled into the yard. Peter ducked inside the building and returned with the camp director.

The man who climbed out of the truck wore a gray shirt and a shiny blue jacket like a state trooper's. A little dark mustache curved above his wide smile. He and Mr. Davis shook hands.

"Ranger Carl Deming," Mr. Davis said, "meet Megan Parnell and Peter Lewis, student counselors. They, too, are concerned about the historical site at Morning Gulch."

"Glad to meet you." Carl shook their hands. "Setting aside that old mining area for posterity was a great plan. I understand the idea started with some kids about your age."

"Yes. Jodi Marsh and her brother and cousin," Megan said.

"Thanks for letting us tag along to the resort site with you," Mr. Davis said. "One of our aims here at outdoor school is to teach good conservation practices. The campers who watched the men at work were quite concerned about what they saw as bad conservation."

"We'll see what's going on," answered the ranger.

He opened the door and flipped the back of the passengerseat forward. Peter and Megan climbed into the backseat of the extended cab pickup.

"A group of professional people with money to invest are behind the resort project," Carl Deming told them, sliding behind the steering wheel. "Besides the main lodge and cabins, they plan a network of hiking and riding trails to hook up with existing Forest Service trails and roads." He started the engine and pulled onto the highway. "They plan to use the trail network for cross-country skiing in the winter."

Megan's stomach twisted. How would the Steincroft cabin fare, unprotected all winter, if people could ski right to it?

Soon Carl turned the truck onto the road they'd passed yesterday. Tall trees crowded on either side. He shifted into four-wheel drive as they bounced over big chunks of broken rock. After a while, he stopped and set the hand brake. They all got out. At the road's edge, pebbles dislodged by their feet skittered over the embankment. They splashed into a stream rushing through a culvert almost big enough to park the truck in.

"Is this the creek from Morning Gulch?" Megan asked.

Ranger Carl nodded. "Yes. It empties into the Chuckawamish across from the school camp property."

Then it *was* the same creek where she'd seen Jeremy James skulking the day she and the campers walked the old railroad grade.

"It's muddier than it should be," Carl continued. "It could be from the rain we've had ..."

" ... or the mud could be coming from the logging operation," Mr. Davis finished.

Peter pulled his camera from under his slicker. Smart move, Megan thought. She'd been too upset over the fight with Willow to even think about bringing hers. Peter shielded the lens from spattering raindrops and snapped a picture.

Carl smiled his wide grin. "Getting the facts on film? Try not to be too conspicuous if you take pictures at the work site."

"That sounds like we're spying!" Before Peter tucked the camera back under his coat he took a picture of them beside the truck. "I'll be careful."

The road swung away from the creek. It looped upward for some distance, then leveled as they came to the clearing where the men were working.

Carl stopped the truck near an expensive new four-wheel drive vehicle that hadn't been there yesterday. Beyond a big pile of logs, they glimpsed the yellow bull-dozer and the flatbed truck. A few yards away, tucked back under some trees, sat the white construction trailer. A long, narrow window flanked either side of its door. Megan thought she saw movement behind one of the windows, but when she looked again she saw nothing. Both Carl and Mr. Davis rolled down their windows. The scream of a chain saw echoed from the hill across the clearing.

Suddenly the noise stopped. Somebody yelled "Timber!" The top of a tall fir swayed. An explosive *C-R-*

A-C-K rent the air as the majestic tree slowly tipped toward them. It fell with an earth-shaking roar into the clearing. Foliage and other debris hung in the air, then rained down onto quivering branches.

"Wow!" exclaimed Peter.

A lump choked Megan's throat. She knew Willow—maybe even Sean—would call her melodramatic for feeling this way. But the trees surrounding the empty place in the forest trembled, as if mourning the giant lying broken on the ground.

Jeb and Stan, two of the men Megan and Peter had met the day before, clambered onto the trunk to cut away the massive boughs with their chain saws. The third calk-booted logger tromped toward the DNR truck from the other side of the clearing. With him came a well-fed older man wearing an expensive woolen jacket and high-laced boots. The newcomer pushed his florid face close to the open window of the pickup. Though the rain had almost stopped, a few drops of water shook from the brim of his hard hat. Megan noticed the hand-stitching on the soft leather gloves that gripped the door. "Yes, sir," the older man said, his voice rough with impatience. "What can we do for you?"

Carl stuck out his hand. "Carl Deming, Department of Natural Resources Forest Practices Coordinator. Mr.—?"

"Doctor. Dr. Arnold James, one of the owners of this project. This is our foreman, Walt Bogart."

Carl introduced Mr. Davis, Megan, and Peter. As Megan said hello, something niggled at the back of her mind. Dr. Arnold James. As in Jeremy James? Hadn't

Miss Loring said Jeremy's father was a doctor?

Mr. Davis spoke. "I'm from the school camp, Dr. James. Your men played an important part in the rescue of a sick child on a camp outing yesterday. We'd like you to know we're all very grateful."

Walt Bogart nodded toward the young people and spoke to Arnold James. "They're the ones I told you about."

"Very good," said the doctor. "Mr. Deming, we're extremely busy. Again I ask, how can we help you?"

"Oh, we'd just like to wander around a little, see how you're coming along."

Dr. James cleared his throat. "This is a hard hat area. We can't be responsible for the safety of your party."

"Of course," said Carl. "We have hard hats, and we'll not hinder you. By the way, do you have your timber harvesting permit on the premises?"

Dr. James glanced at his foreman.

"I'm just getting the office set up but I'll look for it," Walt Bogart said. He headed toward the nearby trailer.

Megan and Peter slid out of the truck behind the ranger and Mr. Davis. Carl pulled hard hats out of a box in the bed of the truck and showed them how to adjust the webbing inside to fit their heads. Then he asked where the lodge and cabins would go.

The doctor pointed toward the slope from which the big tree had been cut. "The buildings will be up there. Here on the flat we'll have the barn and corrals for the horses."

Megan adjusted her hat and put it on. "Could you

take a picture of them working on that big tree?" she whispered to Peter.

"Okay. Stand between me and the others," he muttered, and snapped a quick shot, tucking the camera out of sight again.

Carl Deming led the group over the scarred, muddy ground in the general direction of the stream. Dr. James watched. Suddenly he hurried after them. "I have a map of the plans in my vehicle," he said. "Why don't you come on over and take a look?"

For a busy man, he'd suddenly become very eager to share his time with them, Megan thought.

"Thanks, but I can see it later, if necessary," said Carl. "We'll just walk down to the stream, then after I take a look at your permit, we'll be on our way."

As Megan turned to follow Carl, she looked past the scowling Dr. James, past the loggers on the fallen tree. She saw someone watching from the shelter of the woods. Someone with dark hair and muscular shoulders. Before she could get Peter's attention, the man faded back into the shadows. But she was almost positive that the man was Jeremy James—and she shuddered.

At the stream, the trees which had fallen in the water were gone, except for a few shredded branches scattered around. The brush which normally lined the stream bank had been torn out and mashed into the mud when machinery dragged the logs away.

Carl examined the scarred bank and the churned-up ground, speaking a few notes into a pocket-sized tape recorder. The clear stream curved into the bank, nibbled at the unprotected soil, and swirled it away. Peter changed the film in his camera and took more pictures while Megan tried to stand between him and the workers. She studied the surrounding forest, but the mysterious watcher did not reappear.

Carl dropped the tape recorder into his jacket pocket and pulled out a small booklet. "These are the regulations concerning the streams and their bordering habitats—the Riparian Management Zone. Many people don't know that eighty percent of all birds, animals, and insects spend at least part of their life span in this zone. Besides fish, lots of other wildlife is lost when Riparian Zones are damaged."

Carl slapped the booklet against his palm. "The rules say they are supposed to leave a strip of forest along the stream bank—no disturbance, no vehicles. Let's go see if they've found that cutting permit."

As they headed back, they saw Dr. James and Walt Bogart waiting in front of the office. Walt handed a paper to Carl. He looked it over carefully.

"I can explain the problem with the creek bank," Dr. James said. "We had some faulty communication. The crew cut those trees along the bank by mistake."

"By mistake?" Carl did not smile. He tapped the paper. "The regulations are spelled out right here on your permit." He glanced around the clearing before handing the paper back to Walt. "I'd like to measure that tree you just cut, if you don't mind."

Carl reached under the truck's seat and pulled out the biggest measuring tape Megan had ever seen. The others waited by the truck while Walt and Dr. James walked over to the big tree with Carl. Carl measured its the length and diameter.

"Even though it's private property there are regulations governing which trees may be cut," Mr. Davis said. "He's figuring out the board feet of timber in that tree."

Hoping for a better view of what Carl was doing, Megan stepped up on a stump beside the office trailer. As she turned to suggest that Peter take a picture from her vantage point, she noticed some rectangular pieces of paper the size of index cards scattered over the muddy ground between the building and the stump. They looked clean and new, as if just dropped there.

She hopped down to pick up the first one, turned it over, and gasped. It was a black-and-white photograph, grainy and out of focus. But the subject was clear: a young girl, partially clothed, sitting on a bunk in a cabin. Tamarack cabin. The girl was Soo Yun.

Megan quickly looked around to see if anyone had noticed, then grabbed up the three or four other photos. There was another of Soo Yun, smiling shyly, beside the trunk of a tree. In one, she recognized a girl from another cabin wearing shorts and a skimpy top, posing like a sexy calendar girl. Two shots showed the inside of Megan's cabin with a bit of the half-wall in the foreground and several of the girls getting into their night clothes. She stared at the last picture in disbelief. It was a shot of her, back to the camera but naked from the waist up, laughing over her shoulder at someone not in the picture.

Megan swallowed hard to keep from throwing up. Obviously someone had hidden outside the cabin, spying and taking the horrible pictures. She thought of the film wrapper and the footprints she'd found by the river that second morning at camp. With sinking certainty, she knew who had taken them. Even worse, that person lurked nearby and was probably watching right now.

Well, let him watch. *She* had the pictures, and he would not get them back. She slipped them into her raincoat pocket.

Carl and Dr. James tramped back through the mud to the truck. "People from the county and from the Departments of Fisheries and Wildlife will need to look into what's happening here," Carl said. "I'm shutting you down temporarily."

The doctor drew in his breath. His face turned purple-red. "You can't do that!" he exploded. "We're on an extremely tight schedule!"

Carl motioned for the others to get into the truck. "I don't want to cause difficulty for you and your group, Dr. James. But until you come up with a plan for fixing the damage you've caused to that stream, and until it's clear you're following all the regulations, I can't allow you to continue."

He climbed into the truck, slammed the door, and drove it back onto the road, leaving Dr. James fuming. "He's worried about his pocketbook," Mr. Davis said. "The regulations *are* complicated, but those are intelligent people. They must have thought they could get around the rules."

"Well," said Carl, "after today the good doctor may find more time to listen. How about sending me copies of your photos, Peter? I'd like to have them in my files."

"Sure," Peter agreed. "I'll send them soon as they are developed."

Megan wished they'd stop talking about photos. The pictures in her pocket felt huge and heavy and unclean. She wished she'd never found them.

She unbuckled her seat belt and scooted closer to the front seat. "Mr. Davis, maybe you'd know. Is Jeremy James' father a doctor?"

Mr. Davis swiveled around to look at her. "Yes, I believe he is."

"I think Jeremy is back there, with the loggers," Megan said, her voice shaking.

"I happen to know Soo Yun's parents filed charges against Jeremy last night, and the police interviewed him," Mr. Davis told her. "Of course, that doesn't mean he's in jail yet. Perhaps there wasn't enough evidence to hold him. Or if he was arrested, someone might already have posted his bail."

"And that someone could have been his father, right?" Megan told about seeing Jeremy checking out the muddy creek, where it flowed into the river across from camp, and about his denial that he'd been there. "He probably knew all along what his father was doing and wanted to keep anyone else from finding out."

"That would explain why he siphoned the gas out of the bus too," Peter said.

As they bounced off the logging road onto the highway, Mr. Davis briefly explained to Carl why Jeremy was in trouble.

"Sounds like Dr. James has plenty of problems to deal with right now," Carl said.

"But Megan," Peter interrupted, "What makes you think Jeremy is at the resort site?"

"Someone was in the office when we drove up—I saw a face at the window." To her embarrassment, her voice still shook. "Later I saw someone who looked like Jeremy hiding in the woods."

Peter looked hard at her. "Even if it was Jeremy, why should it make you so upset?"

Mr. Davis also watched her intently.

"Because," she said, choking back a sob and pulling the ugly pictures from her pocket, "I found these by the office."

~~~~~~~~~~~~~~~~~~~~~~~~~~~~

Carl had thanked Megan, Peter, and Mr. Davis for alerting him to the damage at the resort site and dropped them off at Camp Galena.

Mr. Davis hurried directly to his office to phone a detective friend of his at the county Crimes Against Children Unit. "He's going to pull some strings," Mr. Davis assured Megan and Peter. "I told him about these pictures you found. Now that we know he's targeted more than just one child, it will be easier to get an arrest warrant for Jeremy James. The police will be at the resort site before Dr. James and the rest pack up and leave, I hope. With a search warrant too. They'll look for evidence that Jeremy's as involved in child pornography as these pictures seem to indicate."

"I feel so embarrassed and dirty," Megan said. "Who else is going to see those pictures?"

"Don't worry." Mr. Davis' eyes were kind. "The police may want to use some of these as evidence in Soo

Yun's case, but the rest of you shouldn't need to be identified. I hope it helps for you to know that because of your efforts, Megan, Jeremy James will probably never be allowed to work around kids again."

Mr. Davis' words made her feel better, although her heart still felt heavy over the damage at Morning Gulch. There was no way the developers could replace the big trees. If only they could be convinced to disturb the rest of the forest as little as possible.

A group of campers trailed by, following Mr. Edgebert. "I'm supposed to be with them," Peter said. "See you later, Megan."

She pulled her schedule from her jeans pocket to check where she should be. At least the rain had stopped. Later, when the lunch bell rang, Megan ran to Tamarack to drop off her rain gear. The cabin was empty. Uneasily, she remembered Willow and the fight. Sooner or later, she would have to face her.

"Lord, what can I do? It wasn't my fault."

Just love her.

Startled, Megan peered around the room. No, she'd not really *heard* words spoken out loud. But they'd been spoken, in her heart. It was as if all the verses in God's Word talking about Jesus' love were crowding into her mind. "She's not easy to love, Lord," Megan sighed. "But I'll try."

As she turned onto the main trail leading to the mess hall, a familiar voice called her name. Sean jogged up to her. "I haven't seen you all morning. Where've you been?"

Megan told him about their trip to talk to Dr. James and the loggers, leaving out the part about Jeremy.

"You're really taking this thing seriously, aren't you?" he said with his easy grin. "Are you going to work this hard when you're class vice president?"

"I haven't said I want to be vice president yet," Megan told him. "And people have to take ecology seriously now. Later might be too late."

"Yeah, you're right," he said. "Say, I hear you and Willow had quite a battle this morning. That true?"

"Who told you that?" Megan blushed.

"Oh, a little bird. It said you fought about me." He stopped walking and took her hand. "You're cute when you blush."

Megan blushed harder, which made her mad. "You were only a part of it," she said, snatching her hand away and dodging around him. "I hope that little bird didn't gossip all over the camp. It was no big deal."

She marched into the mess hall and plopped into a chair without looking at him. There at the other end of the table sat Willow. The green eyes narrowed, darting from Megan to Sean. Then she tossed her shining hair, pasted a smile on her face, and avoided Megan's eyes.

Megan tried to make her own smile genuine, but inside her emotions felt as tangled as a kitten's ball of yarn. No doubt about it. Being at camp had become a lot more complicated than she'd expected.

The voices of kids and counselors filled the mess hall. As Megan bowed her head and gave thanks for her lunch, her mind still whirled with the morning's events, especially the pressure of Sean's hand on hers and his teasing remark, "You're cute when you blush."

"Megan. Megan, look!" Tikela jiggled her arm. She thrust a folded paper under Megan's nose. On the front was a drawing of Tamarack cabin with the campers on the porch, big tears running down their faces. A caption said, "We all miss you." Inside, a picture of Hanna Joy grinned from her hospital bed. Handwritten messages from her cabin mates surrounded it.

"Nice job, Tikela."

"Will you sign it too?" Tikela held out a pen.

Megan wrote, "I'll never forget our Morning Gulch adventure. Love you!" and added her signature.

"Thank you. Soo Yun says she'll take it to her." Tikela carried it to the other end of the table. Willow scribbled her name.

The girls whispered to each other, shifting uneasy glances between the two student leaders. Megan realized that they all knew about the fight.

When the campers finished eating, Mr. Davis asked the Morning Gulch hikers to remain in the mess hall for a meeting. As the KP crew clattered dishes and wiped the tables, Megan became aware of an argument going on nearby.

"It was her fault!"

"Was not! Your counselor thinks she's so pretty. She doesn't care if she's a good counselor or not."

"Willow's right," snapped the girl whom Megan had told to wear jeans for the hike. "Your counselor tells everyone what to do."

With a sick feeling, Megan realized the campers were carrying on the fight between Willow and her. "Wait a minute." She spoke loudly over the noise. "Listen to me, everyone."

The Tamarack girls turned to face her. Embarrassed, Megan noted that a lot of other people were listening too.

"Willow and I had a fight," she told the girls. "It was a poor way to settle an argument. I'm sorry I wasn't a better example." Megan looked at Willow, who was too surprised to avoid her eyes. "I'm sorry for the things I said, Willow. Will you forgive me?"

Willow stared, then, realizing that everyone was watching her, lowered her eyes. She nodded stiffly.

"Please don't discuss it any more," Megan said to the girls, putting her arms around the chief battlers. "We have only a little time left to enjoy camp. Besides, we've got work to do."

Willow left to join the campers who'd gone to the resource building. Miss Loring called the Morning Gulch hikers together. She talked with them about what they'd learned, then asked for ideas to improve the hike for other groups.

"People should carry whistles in case they get lost," suggested a boy. Miss Loring jotted the suggestion on a rolling whiteboard.

Across the room, one of Peter's campers stood and said, "Make signs to tell about the different trees and plants along the trail."

"And about the marbled mar ... murrelet," said another. "Put a sign where we looked down at the logging, to tell about taking care of streams too."

Soon Miss Loring's list had about a dozen suggestions. "Thank you," she said. "Some of your ideas will make good projects for other Camp Galena campers." They sang a few camp songs, then she dismissed the campers to finish packing to go home. "The buses leave in half an hour," she said.

Soo Yun stopped by Megan and hugged her. "I'm glad you're my friend, Megan. Can I call you sometime?"

"I hope you will." Megan hugged her back.

Soo Yun hurried off, and Megan started after her group, but just outside the building Mr. Davis stopped her. A fine drizzle had started again. "Well, Megan," he said, "We'll miss you. Several people have told me they wish you could be hostess at the Steincroft cabin for the rest of this fall's camping sessions."

"I wish I could too," Megan answered. "Thanks for letting me do it this time."

"Do you suppose you could put the Morning Gulch story on paper so we'd have it for future campers?"

"Oh ... sure! Maybe Jodi Marsh will help. It's really her story," she answered. Megan said good-bye and dashed through the mist to Tamarack cabin. Her girls had already gathered their belongings and left. She grabbed her sleeping bag and duffle. Pausing for a moment, she swept the room with her gaze. No forgotten sneakers or hairbrushes ... only Laurel's cardboard box "night stand" remained to remind her of the lively bunch that had made this cabin home for the past three days.

Footsteps sounded above her head and clattered down the stairs. Willow hesitated when she saw Megan, then hurried on.

"Wait, Willow." Megan ran after her. "I meant what I said earlier. I'm sorry about the fight."

Willow refused to meet her eyes. "Just drop it," she mumbled, not even slowing her stride.

Well, Jesus, Megan thought later as the bus rolled along toward Madrona Bay, I tried to fix it. She made a wry face. You said to love her. You didn't say I had to like her.

~~~~~~~~~~~~~~~~~~~~~

By the time Megan and Peter had sorted their own belongings from the pile beside the bus, Sarah Lewis had arrived with the van. Megan hugged her mother. "Did you miss us?"

"What do you think?" Mrs. Lewis said, hugging back.

In the van, Megan and Peter talked nonstop about their time at Camp Galena.

"Wait a minute." Sarah smiled. "First, are you hungry?"

"I'm always hungry," Peter answered.

"Well, your dad will be late tonight. How'd you like to stop at McDonald's?"

"Great."

"And then could we go to the hospital?" Megan quickly told her mother about Hanna Joy.

Sarah Lewis looked at her watch. "All right."

At McDonald's they got in line to give their orders. "Cheeseburgers for everyone?" Sarah asked.

"Two for me," said Peter. "And a chocolate shake."

As they waited for their orders, a voice behind them said, "Hi." Megan turned to see Jodi Marsh just leaving with a couple of girls. "Be right with you," Jodi said to her friends. "How was Camp Galena, Megan?"

"Oh, great." Megan introduced Jodi to her mom, then moved out of line so they could talk.

"The best part was getting to see Morning Gulch." Megan quickly told Jodi about the hike and how interested the campers had been in the Steincroft cabin and the mine. She told about Hanna Joy getting sick and how they had climbed down the mountain to ask the loggers for help.

"They're building a resort?" Distress swept over Jodi's freckled face. "How can they do that? Morning Gulch will never be the same with buildings and cars and all that so close."

Megan told her about their trip with Carl Deming from the Department of Natural Resources. "He stopped the work until they replant the stream bank. Carl said that other agencies would check on what they're doing too. But I'm afraid they'll find a way to carry on."

Peter joined them with a tray full of food. "I wish there was a way to get the local newspapers interested," Jodi said. "If those developers knew people were watching, maybe they'd back off."

"Oh!" Megan gasped. "Maybe there is. Why couldn't we get a reporter interested in the story? Put public pressure on the developers to do things right?" She remembered Mr. Davis' request for her to write the story of Morning Gulch. She'd wanted to get Jodi's assistance with that, but there wasn't time now. "Jodi, your friends are waiting. Can I call you later?"

"Sure." Jodi wrote her phone number on a napkin and gave it to Megan. "Talk to you soon."

"A reporter!" Peter exclaimed. "Public pressure! Megan, you should be a politician."

~~~~~~~~~~~~~~~~~~~~

On their way to the hospital, Megan thought about Peter's remark. Sean wanted her to be his vice president. But he seemed more interested in what being elected could do for him than for what he could do for the school. Even though she wanted very much to work with him, could she go along with Sean's kind of politics?

The nurse at the desk told Megan where to find Hanna Joy. Her mother and Peter waited in the visitor's lounge while Megan walked down the bare, echoing hall. She peeked through an open door. Hanna Joy sat in bed watching television. When she saw Megan she bounced to her knees, a big smile lighting her face.

"Megan! Soo Yun just left. Her parents brought her right from the bus. Thank you for the card." She indicated Tikela's card sitting on the table. "I love it! And thank you for coming. Tell me all about the rest of the hike."

142

Megan pulled up a chair. "I will. But first, how are you?"

"Oh, I'm fine. I'm still in remission ... I just got too tired, the doctor said. My mom and dad are coming to get me any time now."

"Oh, Hanna Joy, that's wonderful!" Megan gave her a squeeze, knocking her bandanna crooked.

Before Hanna Joy replaced it, she pointed to her head, beaming. "See? Hair."

Megan looked. Sure enough, a silky, blonde fuzz caught the light.

Hanna Joy talked on. "The most exciting thing of all was going up in the air to the helicopter!"

"Miss Loring told us about it. Weren't you scared?"

"Kind of. But the paramedic strapped me in the basket so I couldn't see down. It felt like going up past the trees in an elevator—an elevator that swings back and forth."

Megan told Hanna Joy about asking the loggers to call the paramedics. Then a nurse came in with Hanna Joy's parents. They thanked Megan for helping their daughter, and the girls promised to keep in touch.

As Megan left the room, she felt light and happy. Hanna Joy's leukemia was still in remission. Soo Yun would get help in putting her bad experience behind her. And Morning Gulch? She could only hope their efforts would make a difference.

Saturday afternoon Megan sat in the den, typing into the computer the story she and Jodi had written about the history of Morning Gulch. Someone knocked.

"It's me," said Peter, poking his head in. "I just got back from the photo-finishing place in the mall. Do you want to see my pictures?"

"Sure. First let me print this. Then you can read my story and tell me if I left anything out." She saved what she'd done and clicked on "print." "I got so busy with other things at camp I didn't even finish my first roll of film," she said. "Otherwise you could have taken my pictures in too."

They plopped down on the rug as Peter opened a package of photos. "These are mostly my campers," he said, leafing through shots of kids mugging for the camera.

"They're nice and clear," Megan said, lingering over one of Sean posing in front of his and Peter's cabin. "How did those you took on the hike turn out?"

He opened a second packet. He showed some photos of the hikers zigzagging up the old slide. "And here are the ones I took from the ridge when we first saw the loggers working."

Megan studied the pictures. "The trees they felled into the stream really show up in this one," she said. "Good!"

He opened the last packet with the close-up shots of the damage to the creek bed and of Carl Deming measuring the big fallen tree.

Megan laughed as he showed her a picture of Dr. James scowling at Carl Deming. "I didn't see you take that."

"Dr. James didn't either. He'd have scalped me!" Peter divided the pictures into several piles. "These are the duplicates Carl Deming asked for," he said. "Do you want the extra camp pictures?"

"Yes, thank you," said Megan. "I'm glad you got some of my campers. I love this one of Soo Yun and Hanna Joy giggling."

Megan got up, looking once more at the shot of Sean. "I think I'll put some of these on my wall," she said. She picked up the newly printed Morning Gulch story. "Would you read this now?"

Peter took the pages and read through them. "Good job!" he said. "This ought to be published."

"Thank you." Megan thought a minute. "Maybe I'll print a bunch of copies—for Jodi, and the Historical Society, and anybody else who wants one."

"Oh, Megan, I missed you. Welcome back!" Thuy Nguyen's eyes shone. "Tell me all about Camp Galena."

Megan hung her new brown jacket in their locker and grinned at her friend. "There's so much to tell we'd have to talk all through English class, and I don't think Mrs. Jefferson will allow that. Why don't you see if you can sleep over tonight?"

"Megan! Here you are." She turned to see Sean lean against Willow's locker and smile down at her. "I didn't get to check with you before you disappeared Friday. You still want to go for a Coke this afternoon?"

Thuy touched her arm with a knowing smile. "Let's make it tomorrow night, Megan. See you in class."

Megan looked after Thuy, then back to Sean, flustered. "Sean, what are you talking about?"

Y ou mean I didn't officially ask you?" His grin was apologetic and charming. "You can make it, can't you?"

"Well ..." Megan remembered Miss Chang's request to stop in. "Miss Chang wanted Peter and me to come after school and tell her more about the developers at Morning Gulch. If you want to wait until after that ..."

"Fine. I'll meet you at her room." Sean was off.

Megan's thoughts swirled. She had a real date with Sean Bertram, one of Madrona High's most fantastic boys!

After seventh period, Megan grabbed books and jacket from her locker and dashed to meet Peter outside Miss Chang's classroom. Quickly she told him about her date for that afternoon. "Will you tell Mom where I am, Peter? I'll catch a later bus."

"Okay, if you're sure meeting Sean is what you want."

"Of course it's what I want."

He shrugged. "Go ahead. It's no big deal."

Megan paused with her hand on the doorknob and faced her stepbrother. "You don't like Sean much, do you?"

"It's not that, Megan. But he makes fun of what's

most important to us—our faith."

"What do you mean? Sean's in our youth group ..." Then Megan remembered the teasing remark he'd made when he saw her praying. "Well, maybe he just doesn't really know Jesus yet. Maybe I'll get a chance to tell him ..." Her voice trailed off.

Miss Chang welcomed them and introduced them to a plump young man whose name, she said, was Conner O'Day. "Conner's a reporter for the *Madrona Bay Morning News*. He's a friend of Miss Loring's."

A reporter! Thanks, Lord, Megan thought, amazed. This is exactly what we needed.

"Miss Loring told me about your trip with the Department of Natural Resources ranger to see the developers," Miss Chang continued. "We feel you've uncovered a story the paper might be interested in."

"First, tell me why you were at Morning Gulch," Conner said. So Megan and Peter told him about the school camp, the hike, and their trip to the work site. "Those men own the land. We can't stop them from building a resort there," said Megan. "But they should obey the rules."

"Perhaps," replied Conner O'Day, "a bit of publicity would help persuade them to clean up their act. Of course, I'll need to talk to a few other people to get a balanced report." He paused. "Peter, Miss Chang said you might have some pictures."

Peter unzipped his backpack and pulled out his envelopes of photos. "Here. What do you think?"

The reporter riffled through the photos. "I couldn't have done better myself. Would you let me run a few of these with the story? The paper would pay you."

"Oh, sure."

Conner handed Peter a photo agreement to sign and asked for the identities of the people in the pictures. Then he thanked them and Miss Chang for their help.

As Peter and Megan stood to go, someone knocked at the classroom door. "Come in," called Miss Chang.

Sean leaned in. "Excuse me for interrupting. I was afraid I might have missed Megan."

"We're just finishing." Miss Chang smiled good-bye to the three young people.

In the hall, Peter said, "See you later." He sauntered away, leaving Megan alone with Sean.

Outside, yellowing maple leaves rustled to the sidewalk as she walked beside him toward the fast-food restaurant. She searched for something to say. "I think fall is the nicest season, don't you?"

"I guess I never thought about it," he answered. "Has anyone told you, you look like autumn yourself in that gold-and-brown outfit, with those big brown eyes and sun-kissed cheeks?"

Megan blushed. "Thank you."

Sean certainly knew how to flatter a girl. An image skittered like one of the maple leaves through her thoughts—Sean laughing and talking with Willow. What kind of compliments did he give her?

At the Burgerville's door they stopped. "Want to go inside," he asked, "or should we find a place out here?"

"Oh, let's sit over there in the sunshine," Megan answered, indicating an empty table for two.

"Coke okay?"

Megan nodded. Sean went inside and came out again with two large drinks.

"I went to see Hanna Joy on Friday after we got back," Megan said, unwrapping her straw and plunging it through the ice cubes.

"She all right?"

"She's fine." Megan sipped her drink. "Sean, what do you think will happen with the resort those men want to build?"

"Oh, they'll build it. Why not? It's their land. Besides, where would we be if the first settlers hadn't been able to cut the trees? No cities, no farms, no roads ..."

Megan stared at him. "But don't you think we need to save what's left?"

"Why? People are more important than trees and animals."

"Maybe that's true, but when God put man on the earth, He told him to take care of it. He didn't mean we should use everything up and leave nothing for future generations."

He shrugged. "That's a problem someone else can solve, as far as I'm concerned. Let's talk about more important things."

"What's more important?"

"You. And me."

Megan's eyes widened.

"And the student body elections."

"Oh." Of course. Sean always had more than one reason for everything he did—even asking a girl out.

"Have you decided yet if you'll run for vice president?"

"No ... I'm thinking and praying about it."

"What's with you, Megan? Lots of people would jump at a chance like this."

To be vice president or to work with you? The question was on the tip of Megan's tongue but she held it back.

Sean stared at her quizzically. "I mean it, Megan. Why are you so different?"

"I want to spend my time doing what Jesus wants me to do, Sean. I'm not sure yet that He wants me to run for office."

"You could be vice president and still be a Christian," Sean said. "I go to church too, you know. It's not going to make any difference to my campaign, as long as I keep it fairly quiet."

Did he mean she should be quiet about her faith? Obviously he had going to church and being a Christian confused. But still, those blue eyes gazing into her own did funny things to her insides.

She looked at her watch and hopped up. "The next bus will be here in a few minutes. Thanks for the Coke."

"Welcome. Want me to walk you to the stop?"

"No need. See you tomorrow?"

Sean nodded.

As Megan discarded her drink container, she glanced back. Sean was already talking to a group of kids at another table.

⁓⁓⁓⁓⁓⁓⁓⁓⁓⁓⁓⁓⁓⁓⁓⁓⁓⁓⁓

First thing next morning, Megan and Peter stopped by Miss Chang's room. Several students were clustered around the *Madrona Bay Morning News* spread out on her desk.

"Good morning, Megan, Peter," Miss Chang greeted them. "Have you seen the paper yet?"

Peter yawned. "I'm just barely out of bed," he told her.

Megan joined the group around the desk. "These are your pictures, Peter!"

She skimmed the page. There was a long article by Conner O'Day about Morning Gulch and the conflict over the resort. Beside the article, an enlargement of Peter's photo showed Carl Deming, Megan, and Mr. Davis inspecting the creek bank.

"Wonderful!" she said. "I hope the developers see this."

"They will," Miss Chang said. "And with that publicity, you can be sure they'll be more careful in the future."

Peter, who'd been looking over Megan's shoulder, suddenly jabbed his finger at a short article on the opposite page. "Look at this!"

Megan glanced over, and the headline seemed to leap off the page:

REC DIRECTOR ACCUSED OF INDECENT LIBERTIES WITH CAMPERS

Jeremy James, son of Madrona Bay physician Dr. Arnold James, was arrested Friday afternoon at his father's resort site in the Cascade Mountains. The construction site is near the outdoor education camp where the younger James had worked as recreation director until recent accusations of child molestation.

Detectives from the Crimes Against Children Unit, acting on a tip and armed with a search warrant, raided the site. They discovered quantities of child pornography, including nude photos of children at the camp.

"They got him!" Megan cried. "Oh, I hope this means he'll be locked away somewhere so he can't victimize kids ever again!"

Grinning, she left the room with Peter. She said good-bye to him and headed down the hall toward her locker. She rounded a corner and paused to wait for the crowd of kids blocking the hall to thin out. Familiar broad shoulders loomed just ahead of her. Sean stood next to the wall, his back toward her. She heard Willow speaking.

"Why do you want *her* to be your vice president? You should pick someone popular, someone everybody knows."

"Like you?" Sean said, a teasing smile in his voice. "You're popular and pretty. But I need someone like Megan. A conscientious type, who'll work hard and take the load off my shoulders. With all my other activities, I'm going to be too busy to do a lot of behind-the-scenes work."

Sean's words slammed into her like a sandbag. He didn't want her for herself. He wanted her because ... because he thought she'd do the unglamorous part of his job for him. Stunned, she stood a moment longer. Then, lifting her chin, she stalked past without a glance. Suddenly, she wanted nothing more than to find a hiding place and cry.

"Megan, wait!" It was Sean. He caught up and matched his stride to hers. That confident smile was on his face again. He didn't seem to suspect she'd overheard.

Megan stopped and turned toward him. "Sean, you

remember I told you I needed to be sure student politics was what God wanted me to do?"

He nodded, the smile fading.

"I didn't mean to eavesdrop a minute ago. But I heard what you told Willow, and now I have my answer. You want someone to do your work while you take the credit." She paused, but before he could interrupt she hurried on. "I won't let you take advantage of me, Sean. You're handsome and you're popular. You might get elected president. But I won't be on your team. I won't even vote for you."

Sean stared. As she turned to march toward class, she felt Thuy Nguyen's small hand on her arm.

"Bravo!" Thuy grinned. "I don't know what was behind that speech, but it was one of the best I've ever heard. You sure put him in his place."

A tear spilled onto Megan's cheek. "How could I have thought he was so wonderful?" she asked.

Thuy put her arm around Megan. "Sean has lots of good qualities," she said. "If he'd learn to put Jesus first, he'd be a lot different."

Megan lifted her head and smiled. "You're right. The Holy Spirit can work on Sean Bertram without me."

The girls scooted into their seats as the bell rang. Mrs. Jefferson passed back their What-I-Did-This-Summer essays.

Megan looked at the "A" on her Castaway Island story, her mind still on Thuy's words. Lord, please show Sean what he's missing by leaving You out of his life. Thank You for Camp Galena and for letting me go to Morning Gulch.

Megan smiled as she thought about all that had happened in the past month. Not only had she helped solve the mystery of Thuy's missing brother, but in just the last week alone she'd found mystery and adventure enough to fill a book. With Jesus by her side, how could life be anything but exciting?